"If you're going to be my fake girlfriend, I want one real kiss."

"Not a good idea, Noah."

"Screw good ideas," Noah whispered, his mouth descending to hers. His words moved over her lips, and his eyes bored into hers. "Every time I've seen you since I came back, I've wanted to kiss you. It's bizarre, but I keep wanting to check whether I imagined the power of a furious sea in our kiss. I don't sail much anymore, Jules, and kissing you is the closet I've come for months to belting over a turbulent ocean."

God, how was she supposed to resist? He was all man, so sexy, and in his arms she was the woman she'd always wanted to be. Strong, sexy, powerful, feminine. But they shouldn't be doing this. It so wasn't a good idea...

Noah's mouth on hers kicked that thought away, and all Jules could think about, take in, was that Noah was kissing her.

He made her feel everything she should.

Everything she shouldn't.

* * *

Friendship on Fire is part of the Love in Boston trilogy from Joss Wood!

Dear Reader,

Welcome to the Lockwood Country Club Estate and my new Love in Boston series!

Twins Jules and Darby Brogan, along with their best friend, Dylan-Jane Winston, have grown up on the Lockwood Country Club Estate, and it's a place they all call home. They have lived across the road from the original house on the property, Lockwood House, which has been, up until now, in the hands of a Lockwood for generations. The Lockwood brothers and the Brogans have been friends all their lives, and Noah Lockwood and Jules Brogan have always had a special connection.

Jules and Noah's friendship blew apart after Noah's mom passed away. Noah left Jules without warning and without discussion and started a new life overseas with no explanation. Jules was hurt beyond measure, and the death of her father solidified her belief that love is a destructive emotion and she can't afford to risk her heart. Years pass, and then Noah, now a yacht designer, is forced to return to Boston...

It was so much fun to bring these two emotional, battered people to love, and I hope you enjoy their love story.

Connect with me at www.josswoodbooks.com, on Twitter, @josswoodbooks, and on Facebook, Joss Wood Author.

Happy reading,

Joss

JOSS WOOD

———

FRIENDSHIP ON FIRE

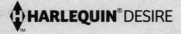
HARLEQUIN® DESIRE

ISBN-13: 978-1-335-97163-0

Friendship on Fire

Copyright © 2018 by Joss Wood

Printed in U.S.A.

HARLEQUIN®
www.Harlequin.com

Joss Wood loves books and traveling—especially to the wild places of Southern Africa. She has the domestic skills of a potted plant and drinks far too much coffee.

Joss has written for Harlequin KISS, Harlequin Presents and, most recently, Harlequin Desire. After a career in business, she now writes full-time. Joss is a member of the Romance Writers of America and Romance Writers of South Africa.

Books by Joss Wood

Harlequin Desire

Convenient Cinderella Bride
The Nanny Proposal

The Ballantyne Billionaires

His Ex's Well-Kept Secret
One Night to Forever
The CEO's Nanny Affair
Little Secrets: Unexpectedly Pregnant

Love in Boston

Friendship on Fire

Visit her Author Profile page at Harlequin.com, or josswoodbooks.com, for more titles.

Prologue

Callie...

As she'd done for nearly thirty years, Callie Brogan kissed her daughter's sable-colored hair, conscious that nothing was guaranteed—not time, affection or life itself so she took every opportunity to kiss and hug her offspring, all seven of them.

God, no, she hadn't birthed them all. Levi and the twins—Jules and Darby—were hers. The Lockwood brothers—Noah, Eli and Ben—were the sons of her heart. Biologically, they belonged to her best friend and neighbor, Bethann Lockwood, who had passed away ten years ago. Dylan-Jane, well, DJ was another child of her heart.

The life Callie had lived back then, as the pampered wife of the stupendously wealthy, successful and most powerful venture capitalist in Boston, was over. Her beloved Ray was gone, too. She'd been a widow for three years now.

Callie was, *gulp*, alone. At fifty-four, it was time to reinvent herself.

So damn scary...

Who was she if she wasn't her kids' mom and her exuberant, forceful husband's wife?

At the moment, she was someone she didn't recognize. She needed to get to know herself again.

"Mom?"

Callie blinked and looked into Jules's brilliant eyes. As always, she caught her breath. Jules had Ray's eyes, that incredible shade of silver blue, incandescently luminous. Callie waited for the familiar wave of grief, and it washed over her as more of a swell than a tsunami.

Damn, Callie missed that man. His bawdy laugh, his strong arms, the sex. Yeah, God, she really missed the sex.

"Mom? Are you okay?" Jules asked, perceptive as always.

Callie waved her words away. She considered herself a modern mom but telling her very adult daughter that she was horny was not something that she'd ever do. So Callie shrugged and smiled. "I'm good."

Jules frowned. "I don't believe you."

Callie looked around and wished Noah—and Eli and Ben—were here. Eli and Ben had excused themselves from Sunday lunch; both were working overtime to restore a catamaran. And Noah was in Italy? Or was it Greece? Cannes? The boy used jet travel like normal people used cars.

Would Noah ever come back home to Boston? The eldest Lockwood boy wasn't one to wear his heart on his sleeve but his stepdad's actions after Bethann's death had scarred him. He had far too much pride to show how wounded he was, to admit he was lost and lonely and hurt. Like Bethann, he saw emotion and communicating his fears as a failure and a weakness.

Noah's independence frustrated Callie but she'd never stopped loving the boy…the man. Noah was in his midthirties now.

Her own son, Levi, sat down on the bigger of the two leather couches and placed his glass of whiskey on the coffee table. "Right, Mom, what's the big news?"

Callie took her seat with Jules next to her, on the arm of the chair. Darby and the twins' best friend, DJ, bookended Levi.

Jules rubbed her hand up and down Callie's back. "What is it, Mom?"

Well, here goes. "Last Tuesday was three years since your dad died."

"We know, Mom," Darby murmured, her elegant fingers holding the stem of her wineglass.

"I've decided to make some changes."

Jules lifted her eyebrows, looking skeptical. Jules, thanks to Noah's desertion and Ray's sudden death, wasn't a fan of impetuous decisions or change. "Okay. Like…?"

Callie looked out the picture windows to the lake and the golf course beyond. "Before you were all born, Bethann's father decided to turn Lockwood Estate into an exclusive gated community, complete with a golf course and country club. Your dad was one of the first people to buy and build on this estate and this house is still, apart from Lockwood itself, one of the biggest in the community."

Her kids' faces all reflected some measure of frustration at the history lesson. They'd lived here all their lives; they'd heard it all before. "It's definitely too big for me. The tenants renting the three-bedroom we own on the other side of the estate have handed in their notice. I'm going to move into that house."

Callie could see the horror on their faces, saw that they didn't like the idea of losing their family home. She'd reassure them. "When I die, this house will come to you, Levi, but I think you should take possession of it now. I've heard each of you talk of buying your own places. It doesn't make sense to buy when you have this one, Levi. The twins can move in here while they look for a property that suits them. This house has four bedrooms, lots of communal space. It's central, convenient, and you'd just have to pay for the utilities."

"Move in with Levi? Yuck," Darby said, as Callie expected her to. But Callie caught the long look her daughter exchanged with her twin sister, Jules, and smiled at their excitement.

Callie knew what was coming next...

"DJ could move into the apartment over the garage," Jules suggested, excitement in her eyes.

She loved this house; they all did. And why wouldn't they? It was spacious, with high ceilings and wooden floors, an outdoor entertainment area and a big backyard. It was close to Lockwood Country Club's private gym, which they all still used. The Tavern, the pub and Italian restaurant attached to the country club, was one of her kids' favorite places to meet, have a drink. The boys played golf within the walls of the pretty, green estate where they were raised, as often as their busy schedules allowed.

It was home.

"I don't want to live with my sisters, Mom. It was bad enough sharing a childhood with them," Levi said.

He was lying, Callie could tell. Levi adored his sisters and this way, he could vet who they dated without stalking them on social media. Levi's protective streak ran a mile long.

"It's a good solution. This way, you don't have to rent while you're looking to buy and, Levi, since I know you and Noah sank most of your cash into that new marina, it'll be a while before your bank account recovers."

Callie wrinkled her nose. Levi probably still had a few million at his fingertips. They were one of Boston's wealthiest families.

Levi shook his head. "Mom, we appreciate the offer, but you do know that we are all successful and you don't need to worry about us anymore?"

She was *Mom*, Callie wanted to tell him. She'd always be *Mom*. One day they'd understand. She'd always worry about them.

"Are you sure you want to move into the house on Ennis Street?" Jules asked.

Absolutely. There were too many ghosts in this house, too many memories. "I need something new, something different. Dad is gone but I'm still standing and I've made the decision to reinvent my life. I have a bucket list and so many things I want to do by the time I turn fifty-five."

"That's in ten months," Darby pointed out.

Callie was so aware, thank you very much.

"What's on the bucket list, Mom?" Jules asked, amused.

Callie smiled. "Oh, the usual. A road trip through France, take an art class, learn how to paint."

Jules sent her an indulgent smile. God. Jules would probably fall off her chair if Callie told her that a one-night stand, phone sex, seeing a tiger in the wild, bungee jumping and sleeping naked in the sun were also on her to-do list. Oh, and she definitely wouldn't tell them that her highest priority was to help them all settle down…

She wasn't hung up on them getting married. No, sometimes marriage, like her best friend's, wasn't worth the paper the license was written on.

Callie wanted her children to find their soft place to fall, the person who would make their lives complete.

But, right now, Callie wanted Noah home, back in Boston, where he belonged.

How was she supposed to get him to settle down when he was on the other side of the world?

One

Noah...

Noah pushed his hand into her thick hair and looked down into those amazing eyes, the exact tint of a new moon on the Southern Ocean. Her scent, something sexy but still sweet, drifted off her skin and her wide mouth promised a kiss that was dark and delectable. His stupid heart was trying to climb out of his chest so that it could rest in her hand.

Jules pushed her breasts into his chest and tilted her hips so that her stomach brushed his hard-as-hell erection...

This was Jules, his best friend.

Thought, time, the raucous sounds of the New Year's

party receded and Jules was all that mattered. Jules with her tight nipples and her tilted hips and her silver-blue eyes begging him to kiss her.

He'd make it quick. Just one quick sip, a fast taste. He wouldn't take it any further. He couldn't. He wanted to, desperately, but there were reasons why he had no right to place his hand on her spectacular ass, to push his chest into her small but perfect breasts.

One kiss, that's all he could have, take.

Noah touched his lips to hers and he fell, lost in her taste, in her scent. For the first time in months his grief dissipated, his confusion cleared. As her tongue slid between his teeth, his responsibilities faded, and the decisions he'd been forced to make didn't matter.

Jules was in his arms and she was kissing him and the world suddenly made sense...

He was about to palm her beautiful breasts, have her wrap her legs around his hips to rock against her core when hands gripped his shoulders, yanked his hair.

Surprised, he stumbled back, fell onto his tailbone to see Morgan and his dad looking down at him, laughing their asses off. His eyes bounced to Jules and tears streaked her face.

"Bastard!" Morgan screamed.

"That's my boy," Ethan cooed. "Blood or not, you are my son."

And Jules? Well, Jules just cried.

Another night, the same recurring dream. Noah Lockwood punched the comforter and the sheets away, unable to bare the constricting fabric against his heated skin. Draping one forearm across bent knees, Noah ran a hand behind his neck. Cursing, he fumbled for the glass of water on the bedside table, grimacing at the handprint his sweat made on the deep black comforter.

Noah swung his legs off the side of the large bed, reached for a pair of boxers on the nearby chair and yanked them on. He looked across the bed and Jenna—a friend he occasionally hooked up with when he was in this particular city—reached over to the side table and flipped on the bedside light. She checked her watch before shoving the covers back, muttered a quick curse and, naked, started to gather her clothes.

"Do you want to talk about it?" she asked.

Hell, no. He rarely opened up to his brothers or his closest friends, so there was no chance he'd talk to an infrequent bed buddy about his dream. Without a long explanation Jenna wouldn't understand, and since Noah didn't do explanations, that would never happen. Besides, talking meant examining and facing his fears, confronting guilt and dissecting his past. That would be *amusing*…in the same way an electric shock to his junk would be *nice*.

He tried, as much as possible, not to think about the past…

Noah walked over to the French doors that opened to the balcony. Pushing them open, he sucked in the briny air of the cool late-autumn night. Tinges of a new morning peeked through the trees that bordered the side and back edges of the complex.

He loved Cape Town, and enjoyed his visits to the

city nestled between the mountains and the sea. It was beautiful, as were Oahu or Cannes or Monaco. But it wasn't home. He missed Boston with an intensity that sometimes threatened to drop him to his knees. But he couldn't go back...

The last time he left it nearly killed him and that wasn't an experience he wanted to repeat.

Noah accepted Jenna's brief goodbye kiss and walked her to the door. Finally alone, he grabbed a T-shirt from the chair behind him and yanked it over his head and, picking up his phone, walked onto the balcony, then perched lightly on the edge of a sturdy morris chair.

The dream's sour aftertaste remained and he sucked in long, clean breaths, trying to cleanse his mind. Because his nightmares always made him want to touch base with his brothers, he dialed Eli's number, knowing he was more likely to answer than Ben.

"Noah, I was just about to call you." Despite being across the world in Boston, Eli sounded like he was in the next room.

Noah heard the worry in Eli's voice and his stomach swooped.

"What's up?" he asked, trying to project confidence. He was the oldest and although he was always absent, his hand was still the one, via phone calls and emails, steering the Lockwood ship. Actually, that wasn't completely true; Levi buying into the North Shore marina and boatyard using the money he inherited from Ray allowed Noah to take a step back. Eli and Ben were a little hotheaded and prone to making impulsive decisions but

Levi wasn't. Noah was happy to leave the day-to-day decisions in Levi's capable hands.

"Callie called us earlier—a for-sale sign has gone up at Lockwood."

"Ethan's selling the house?" Noah asked.

"No. He's selling everything. Our childhood home, the land, the country club, the golf course, the buildings. He's selling the LCC Trust and that includes everything on the estate except for the individually owned houses."

Noah released a low, bullet-like curse word.

"Rumor has it that he needs cash again."

"Okay, let me assimilate this. I'll call you back in a few."

Noah sucked in his breath and closed his eyes, allowing anger and disappointment to flow through him. Ten years ago he'd taken the man he called Dad, a man he adored and whom he thought loved him, to court. After his mom's death he discovered that the marriage that he'd thought was so perfect had been pure BS. The only father he'd ever known, the man he placed on a pedestal was, he discovered, a serial cheater and a spendthrift.

Stopping Ethan from liquidating the last of Lockwood family assets, passed down through generations of Lockwoods to his mom—a legacy important enough to his mom for her to persuade both their biological dad and then their stepdad to take her maiden name—meant hiring expensive legal talent.

Noah ran his hand over his eyes, remembering those bleak months between his mother's death and the court judgment awarding the Lockwood boys the waterfront marina and the East Boston boatyard and Ethan the Lockwood Country Club, which included their house, the club facilities, the shops and the land around it. Ethan was also awarded the contents of the house and the many millions in her bank accounts. All of which, so he'd heard, he'd managed to blow. On wine, women and song.

Fighting for his and his brothers' inheritance had been tough, but he'd been gutted by the knowledge that everything he knew about his mom and Ethan, the facade of happiness they'd presented to the world, had been a sham. A lie, an illusion. By cheating on his mom and choosing money over them, Ethan had proved that he'd never loved any of them.

Why hadn't he seen it, realized that his dad was actually a bastard, that every "I love you" and "I'm proud of you" had been a flat-out lie? Faced with proof of his father's deceit, he'd decided that love was an emotion he couldn't trust, that marriage was a sham, that people, especially the ones who professed to love him, couldn't be trusted.

And Morgan's actions had cemented those conclusions.

The year it all fell apart, he'd spent the Christmas season with Morgan and her parents. Needing something to dull the pain after her parents retired for the night, he'd tucked into Ivan Blake's very expensive whiskey and dimly recalled Morgan prattling on about marriage and a commitment. Since he'd been blitzed and because she'd had her hand in his pants, he couldn't remember what was discussed...

The following day—feeling very un-Christmassy on Christmas morning thanks to a hangover from hell—he'd found himself accepting congratulations on their engagement. He'd tried to explain that it was a mistake, wanted to tell everyone that he had no intention of getting married, but Morgan had looked so damn happy and his head had been on the point of exploding. His goal had been to get through the day and when he had Morgan on her own, he'd backtrack, let her down gently and break up with her as he'd intended to do for weeks. He'd had enough on his plate without dealing with a needy and demanding girlfriend.

Yet somehow, Ivan Blake had discerned his feet were frozen blocks of ice thanks to his sudden engagement to his high-maintenance daughter. Ivan had pulled him into his study, told him that Morgan was bipolar and that she was mentally fragile. Being a protective dad, he'd done his research and knew Noah was a sailor, one of the best amateurs in the country. He also knew Noah wanted to turn pro and needed a team to sail with, preferably to lead.

Ivan had been very well-informed; he'd known of Noah's shortage of cash, his sponsorship offers and that there were many companies wanting to be associated with the hottest sailing talent of his generation.

Ivan had known Noah didn't want to marry Morgan...

He'd said as much and that statement was followed by a hell of an offer. Noah would receive a ridiculous amount of money to sail a yacht of his choice on the pro circuit. But the offer had come with a hell of a proviso...

All Noah had to do was stay engaged to Morgan for two years, and Ivan would triple his highest sponsorship offer. Noah's instant reaction had been to refuse but, damn...three times his nearest offer? That was a hell of a lot of cash to reject. It would be an engagement in name only, Ivan had told him, a way for Morgan to save face while he worked on getting her mentally healthy. Noah would be out of the country sailing and he only needed to send a few emails and make a couple of satellite telephone calls a month.

Oh, and Ivan had added that he had to stay away from Jules Brogan. Morgan felt threatened by his lifelong friendship with Jules and it caused her extreme distress and was a barrier to her getting well.

A week later he'd forgotten that proviso when he kissed the hell out of Jules on New Year's Eve...the kiss he kept reliving in his dreams.

Not going there, not thinking about that. Besides, thinking about Jules and Morgan wasn't helping him with this current problem: Ethan was selling his mom's house, his childhood home and the land that had been in his family for over a hundred and fifty years. That house had been the home of many generations of Lockwoods, and he'd be damned if he'd see it leave the family's hands. His grandfather had built the country club and was its founding member. His mom had been CEO of the club and estate, had kept a watchful eye on the housing development, limiting the estate to only seventy houses to retain the wide-open spaces.

Think, Noah, there's something you're missing.

Noah tapped his phone against his thigh, recalling the terms of the court settlement. Yeah, that's what had been bugging him...

He hit Redial on his phone and Eli answered. "In terms of the court settlement, Ethan has to give us the opportunity to buy the trust before he can put it on the open market."

"I don't remember that proviso," Eli said.

"If he wants to sell, he has to give us three months to buy the property. He also has to sell it to us at twenty percent below the market value."

Noah heard Eli's surprised whistle. "That's a hell of a clause."

"We had an expensive lawyer and I think it's one Ethan has accidentally on purpose forgotten."

"Then I'll contact our lawyer to enforce the terms of the settlement. But, No, even if we do get the opportunity to buy the trust—"

"We *will* get the opportunity," Noah corrected.

"—the asking price is enormous, even with the discount. It's a historic, exceptional house on a massive tract of land. Not to mention the club, the buildings, the facilities. The golf course. We're talking massive money. More than Ben and I can swing."

Noah considered this for a moment. "We'd have to mortgage it."

"The price to us should be around a hundred million," Eli said, his tone skeptical.

"We'd need to raise twenty percent." Under normal circumstances he would never be making a financial decision without a hell of a lot more due diligence. At the very least, he'd know whether the trust generated enough funds to cover the mortgage. He didn't care. This was Lockwood Estate and it was his responsibility to keep it in the family.

"Ben and I recently purchased a fifty-foot catamaran which we are restoring and that's sucked up our savings. We'll be finishing it up in a month or two and then we'll have to wait a few weeks to sell it. Even if it does sell quickly, the profit won't cover our share of the twenty-million deposit. Do you have twenty mil?"

"Not lying around. I invested in that new marina at the Boston waterfront with Levi. I'll sell my apartment in London, it's in a sought-after area and it should move quickly. I'll also sell my share in a business I own in Italy. My partner will buy me out. That would raise eight million."

"Okay. Twelve to go. Ben and I have about a million each sitting in investments we can liquefy."

Thank God his brothers were on board with this plan, that saving Lockwood Estate meant as much to them as it did to him. He couldn't do it without them. Noah ran through his assets. "I have three mil invested. That leaves seven. Crap."

Noah was silent for a long minute before speaking. "So, basically we're screwed."

Damn, his head was currently being invaded by little men with very loud jackhammers.

Eli cleared his throat. "Not necessarily. I heard that Paris Barrow wants to commission a luxury yacht and is upset because she has to wait six to ten months to get it designed. If you can put aside your distaste for designing those inelegant floating McMansions as you call them, I could set up a meeting."

"What's the budget?"

"From what I heard, about sixty million. What are your design fees? Ten percent of the price? That's six mil and I'm sure we can scrounge up another million between us. Somehow."

Noah thought for a moment. He had various projects in the works but none that would provide a big enough paycheck to secure the house. Designing a superyacht would. At the very least he had to try. Noah gripped the bridge of his nose with his forefinger and thumb and stepped off the cliff. "Set up a meeting with your client's friend. Let's see where it goes."

"She's a megawealthy Boston grande dame, and designing for her would mean coming back home," Eli said softly.

Yeah, he got that. "I know."

Noah disconnected the call and stared down at his bare feet. He was both excited and terrified to be returning to the city he'd been avoiding for the past ten years. Boston meant facing his past, but it also meant reconnecting and spending time with Levi, Eli and Ben, DJ, and Darby.

And Callie. God, he'd missed her so much.

But Boston was synonymous with Jules, the only person whom he'd ever let under his protective shell. His best friend until he'd mucked it all up by kissing her, ignoring her, remaining engaged to a woman she intensely disliked and then dropping out of her life.

She still hadn't forgiven him and he doubted that she ever would.

Jules...

Jules frowned at the for-sale sign that had appeared on the lawn of Lockwood House and swung into the driveway of her childhood home—and her new digs— and slammed on the brakes when she noticed a matte black Ducati parked in her usual space next to the detached garage. Swearing, she guided her car into the tiny space next to it and cursed her brother for parking what had to be his latest toy in her space.

Jules looked at the for-sale sign again. She was surprised that the Lockwood boys would let the house go out of their family but, as she well knew, maintaining a residence the size of the houses on this estate cost an arm and a leg and a few internal organs. Jules shoved her fist into the space beneath her rib cage to ease the burn. She'd spent as much time in that house as she had her own, sneaking in and out of Noah's bedroom. But that was back in the days when they were still friends, before he'd met Morgan and before he'd spoiled everything by kissing her senseless.

It had been a hell of a kiss and that was part of the problem. If it had been a run-of-the-mill, *meh* kiss, she could brush it aside, but it was still—*aargh!*—the kiss she measured all other kisses against. Passionate, sweet, tender, hot.

Pity it came courtesy of her onetime best friend and an all-around jerk.

Jules used her key to let herself into the empty house. It was still early, just past eight in the morning, but her siblings would've left for work hours ago. Thanks to efficient workmen and an easy client, her Napa Valley project had gone off without a hitch and as a result, she'd finished two weeks early, which was unexpectedly wonderful. Since winning Boston's Most Exciting Interior Designer award five months ago, she'd been running from one project to another, constantly in demand. For the next few days, maybe a week, she could take it a little easier: sleep later, go home earlier, catch her breath. Chill.

God, she so needed to chill, to de-stress and to rest her overworked mind and body. Despite her business-class seat, she was stiff from her late-night cross-country flight. Jules pulled herself up the wooden stairs, instinctively missing the squeaky floorboards that used to tell a wide-awake parent, or curious sibling, she was taking an unauthorized leave from the house.

Parking her rolling suitcase outside her closed bedroom door, and knowing the house was empty, Jules headed for the family bathroom at the end of the hall, pulling her grubby silk T-shirt from her pants and up and over her head. Opening the door to the bathroom, she tossed the shirt toward the laundry hamper in the corner and stepped into the bathroom.

Hot steam slapped her in the face. A second later she registered the heavy and familiar beat of the powerful shower in the corner of the room. Whipping around and expecting to see Darby or DJ, her mouth fell open at the—God, let's call it what it was—*vision* standing in the glass enclosure.

Six feet four inches of tanned skin gliding over defined muscles, hair slicked off an angles-and-planes face, brown eyes flecked with gold. A wide chest, lightly dusted with blond hair and a hard, ridged stomach. Sexy hip muscles that drew the eye down to a thatch of darker hair and a, frankly, impressive package. A package that was growing with every breath he took.

Noah...

God, Noah was back and he was standing in her shower looking like Michelangelo's *David* on a very, very good day.

Jules lifted her eyes to his face and the desire in his gaze caused her breath to hitch and all the moisture in her mouth to disappear. Jules swallowed, willed her feet to move but they remained glued to the tiled floor. She couldn't breathe. She couldn't think. All she wanted to do was touch. Since that was out of the question— God, she hadn't seen him in ten years, she couldn't just jump him!—she just looked, allowing her eyes to feast.

Noah. God. In her bathroom. Naked.

Without dropping his eyes from hers, Noah switched

off the water and pushed his hair off his face. Opening the door to the shower cubicle, he stepped out onto the mat and placed his hands on his narrow hips. Jules dropped her gaze and, yep, much bigger than before. Strong, hard...

Were either of them ever going to speak, to turn away, to break this crazy, passion-saturated atmosphere? What was *wrong* with them?

Jules was trying to talk her feet into moving when Noah stepped up to her and placed a wet hand on her cheek, his thumb sliding across her lower lip. He smelled of soap and shampoo and hot, aroused male. Lust, as hot and thick as warm molasses, slid into her veins and pooled between her legs. Keeping her hands at her sides, she looked up at Noah, conscious of his erection brushing the bare skin above the waistband of her pants, her nipples stretching the fabric of her lace bra.

Noah just stared at her, the gold flecks in his eyes bright with desire, and then his mouth, that sexy, sexy mouth, dropped onto hers. His hands slid over her bare waist and down her butt, pulling her into his wet, hard body. Jules gasped as his tongue flicked between the seam of her lips and she opened up with no thought of resistance.

It was an exaggerated version of the kiss they'd shared so long ago. This was a kiss on steroids, bold, hotter and wetter than before. Noah's arms were stronger, his mouth more demanding, his intent clear. His hand moved across her skin with confidence and control, settling on her right breast. He pulled down the cup of her bra, and then her breast was pressed into his palm, skin on skin. She whimpered and Noah growled, his thumb teasing her nipple with rough, sexy strokes.

Jules lifted her hands to touch him, wanting to feel those ridges of his stomach on her fingertips, wrap her hand around his—

Holy crap! What the hell? Jules jerked away from him, lifting her hands up when he stepped toward her, intent on picking up where they left off.

Jules slapped her open hand against his still-wet chest and pushed him back. Furious now, she glared up at him. "What the hell, Lockwood? You do not walk back into my life and start kissing me without a damn word! Did you really think that we would end up naked on the bathroom floor?"

"I'm already naked." Noah looked down at her flushed chest, her pointed nipples and her wet-from-his-kiss mouth. "And, yeah, it definitely looked and felt like we were heading in that direction."

Jules opened her mouth to blast him and, flummoxed, couldn't find the words. "I— You— Crap!"

Noah reached behind her for a towel and slowly, oh, so slowly, wrapped it around his hips. He had the balls to smile and Jules wanted to slap him silly. "So, how much does it suck to know that the attraction hasn't faded?"

Jules glared at him, muttered a low curse and turned on her heel and walked toward the open door.

"Jules?"

Jules took her time turning around. "What?"

Noah grinned, his big arms folded across his chest. "Hi. Good to see you."

Jules did her goldfish impression again and, shaking her head, headed to her bedroom. Had that really happened? Was she hallucinating? Jules looked down and saw that the fabric of her bra was wet, water droplets covered her shoulders and ran down her stomach.

Nope, she wasn't dreaming the sexiest dream ever. Noah was back and this was her life.

So this was her punishment for finishing a project early?

Unfair, Universe. Because all she wanted to do was catch a plane back to Napa Valley and Jules hunted for a reason to return to the project she'd just wrapped up. Jules ran through her mental checklist and, dammit, she'd definitely covered all her bases. The workmanship was exemplary, the client was ecstatic and his check was in the bank. There wasn't the smallest reason to haul her butt out of this house and fly back to California.

Balls!

After three months in California she'd desperately wanted to come home, to unpack the boxes stacked against the wall and to catch up with Darby and DJ, her best friends but also her business partners. Darby, her twin, was Winston and Brogan's architect. Jules was the interior designer, and DJ managed the business end of their design and decor company. She spoke to both of them numerous times a day but she wanted to hug them, to be a part of their early-morning meetings instead of Skyping in, to share an icy bottle of wine at the end of the day.

Jules scowled. It was very damn interesting to note that during any one of those many daily conversations one of them could've told her that Noah was back in Boston.

Five words, not difficult. "Noah is back in Boston."

Or even better: "Noah is back in Boston, living in our house."

He was tall and built and it wasn't like they could've missed him!

Jules sat down on the edge of her bed, her feet bouncing off something unfamiliar. Looking down, she saw a pair of men's flat-heeled, size thirteen boots. Lifting her head, she looked around her bedroom. A man's shirt lay over the back of her red-and-white-checked chair, a leather wallet and a phone were on her dressing table. No doubt Noah's clothes were in her closet, too. Noah was not only back in her life, he'd moved into her bedroom and, literally, into her bed.

Jules frantically pushed the buttons on her phone, cursing when neither Darby nor DJ answered her call. She left less-than-happy messages on their voice mails and she was about to call Levi—who hadn't shared the news either—when her phone vibrated with an incoming call.

"Mom, guess what I found in the house when I got home a little while ago?" Jules asked, super sarcastic. "Guess you didn't know that Noah was home either, huh?"

"Damn, you found him."

In the shower, gloriously, wonderfully naked. *Spectacularly naked and I must've looked at him like I wanted to eat him up like ice cream because, before saying a damn word, he kissed the hell out of me.* "Yeah, I found Noah."

"I told your siblings to tell you," Callie said.

Hearing a noise coming from her mom's phone, Jules frowned. "Where are you?"

"At a delightful coffee shop that's just opened up next to the gym at LCC," Callie replied. "Amazing ambience and delicious coffee—"

"And the owner is really good-looking!" A deep voice floated over the phone and was quickly followed by Callie's flirty laugh. Wait…what? Her mom was flirting?

"Is he?" Jules asked, intrigued enough to briefly change the subject.

"Is he what?" Callie replied, playing dumb.

Really, they were going to play this game? "Good-looking, Mom."

"I suppose so. But too young and too fit for me."

"I'll admit to the fit but not to the too young. What's ten years?" the cheerful voice boomed. "Tell your mom to accept a date from me!"

Well, go, Mom! Despite her annoyance at her family in general, Jules laughed, listening as her mom shushed the man. "Maybe you should take the guy up on his offer. Might be fun."

"I'm not discussing him with you, Jules," Callie said, and Jules was sure she could hear her blushing.

Since Callie normally shared everything with her daughters, Jules knew this man had her unflappable mom more flustered than she cared to admit. Now, that was interesting. Before Jules could interrogate her further, Callie spoke. "So, how do you feel about Noah being back in Boston?"

Sidewinded. Horny. Crazy. Flabbergasted.

Not wanting her mom to know how deeply she was affected by this news—hell, the world was Jell-O beneath her feet—Jules let out an exasperated laugh. "It's not a big deal, Mom. Noah is entitled to come home."

"Oh, please, you've been dreading this day for years."

Jules stared down at the glossy wooden floors beneath her feet. "Don't be ridiculous, Mother."

"Jules, you've been terrified of this day because you'll no longer be able to leave your relationship with Noah in limbo. Seeing him again either means cutting him out of your life for good or forgiving him."

"There's nothing to forgive him for." Okay, she had a couple of minor issues with that gorgeous, six-foot-plus slab of defined muscles. Things like him getting engaged to a woman he didn't love and kissing her on New Year's Eve while he was engaged. And then for remaining engaged to Morgan, disappearing from her life without an explanation—she was still furious that he dropped out of college without finishing his degree—and not trying to reconnect with her when he and Morgan had finally called it quits.

In the space of seven years, the two men she loved the most, her best friend and her dad, had dropped out of her life without rhyme, reason or explanation. Her dad had been healthy, too healthy to be taken by a massive heart attack but that was exactly what happened.

Jules doubted there was a reasonable explanation for Noah abandoning her and their lifelong friendship, for not being there at her dad's funeral to hold her hand through the grief.

Okay, maybe that last one wasn't fair; Noah had been in the middle of his last race as a professional sailor at the time.

"No more coffee for me, Mason," Callie said, snapping Jules out of her wayward thoughts.

She grabbed her mom's words like a lifeline. "Mason is a nice name. Is he hot? If he's too young for you, can I meet him?"

"He's far too old for you and not your type." Well, that was a quick reply…and a tad snappy. Did her mom have the hots for Coffee Guy? And why not? It was time she started living for herself again.

"I don't have a type, Mom," Jules replied, and she didn't. She dated men of all types and ethnicities but none of them stuck. She didn't need a psych degree to know that losing the two men she loved and trusted the most turned her into a card-carrying, picket-sign-holding commitment-phobe.

"Of course you do—your type is blond and brown-eyed and has a body that would make Michelangelo weep."

She hadn't said anything about Michelangelo, had

she? How did her mom know that? "Why do you say that?"

"I'm old, not dead, Jules. The boy is gorgeous."

Noah, wet and naked, flashed behind her eyes. *Goddammit*. Like she needed reminding.

"You need to deal with him, Jules. This situation needs to be resolved."

Why? Noah had made his feelings about her perfectly clear when he dropped out of her life. She'd received nothing from him but the occasional group email he sent to the whole clan, telling them about his racing and, after he retired from sailing, his yacht design business. He didn't mention anything personal, instead sharing his witty and perceptive observations about the places he visited and the people he met.

His news was interesting but told Jules nothing about his thoughts and feelings and, once having had access to both, she wasn't willing to settle for so little, so she never bothered to reply. For someone who'd had as much of his soul as he could give, she'd needed more, dammit…

"Mom. God, just butt out, okay?"

There was silence on the other end of the phone but Jules ignored it, knowing that it was her mom's way of showing her disapproval. "Mom, the silent treatment won't work. This is between Noah and me. Stay out of it."

Jules rubbed the back of her neck, feeling guilty at snapping. Her mother had mastered the art of nagging by remaining utterly silent. How did she do that? How?

"Mom, I know you love me but I need you to trust me to do what's best with regard to Noah." Not that she had any bright ideas except to avoid him.

"The problem, my darling, is that you and Noah are so damn pigheaded! Sort it out, Jules. I am done with this cold war."

Jules heard the click that told her Callie had disconnected the call and stared at her phone, bemused. Her mom rarely sounded rattled and considered hanging up to be the height of rudeness. But as much as she loved her mother, she was an adult and had to run her life as she saw fit. That meant leaving her relationship with Noah in the past, where it belonged.

Jules looked up, waited for the lightning strike—her mom, she was convinced, had a direct line to God—and when she remained unfried, she sighed. What to do?

Her first instinct was to run...

Jules heard the bathroom door open and, hearing Noah's footsteps, headed down the hallway in her direction, flew to her feet. Grabbing her bag off the bed, she pulled it over her shoulder and hurried to the door. She pulled it open and nearly plowed into Noah, still bare-chested, still with only a towel around his waist. *Do not look down, do not get distracted. Just push past him and leave...*

"I'm going out, but by the time I return, I want you and your stuff out of my room," Jules stated in the firmest voice she could find.

"Levi said that you were away for another two weeks. He insisted I stay here when he picked me up from the airport yesterday. I'll find a hotel room or bunk on the *Resilience*."

His forty-foot turn-of-the-century monohull that he kept berthed at the marina. The yacht, commissioned by his great-great-grandfather was his favorite possession. It was small but luxurious, and Noah would always choose sleeping on the *Resilience* over a hotel.

"How long are you staying?" She needed to know when her life was going to go back to normal. With a date and a time, the Jell-O would, hopefully, solidify into hard earth.

"I'm not sure. A month? Maybe two?"

Great. She was in for four to eight weeks of crazy. Like her life wasn't busy and stressful enough. Jules rubbed her forehead with her fingers. God, she did not need to deal with this now. Today. Ever. Seeing him created a soup of emotion, sour and sticky. Lust, grief, hurt, disappointment, passion…

All she wanted to do was step into his arms and tell him that she'd missed him so damn much, missed the boy who'd known her so well. That she wanted to know, in a carnal way, the man he was now.

Jules shook her head and pushed past him, almost running to the stairs. *Sort it out, Mom?*

Much, much easier said than done.

Two

Callie...

After a brief and tense conversation with Levi, Callie dropped her forehead to the table and banged her head on the smooth surface. Levi reluctantly admitted to her that none of them told Jules that Noah was back. Nor had they informed her that Noah was sleeping in Jules's bedroom at her old house.

Really, and these people called themselves adults? *Aargh!*

The whisper of a broad hand skated over her hair and she lifted her head a half inch off the table to glare at Mason. With his dark brown hair showing little gray, barely any lines around his denim-blue eyes and his still-hard body, the owner of the new coffee shop looked closer to forty than to the forty-five he claimed to be. Yes, he was sexy. Yes, he was charming, but why, oh, why—in a room filled with so many good-looking women, most of them younger, slimmer and prettier than her—was he paying her any attention?

Mason slid a latte under her nose and took the empty seat across from her. Callie glared at him, annoyed that he made her feel so flustered. And, holy cupcakes, was that lust curling low in her now-useless womb? "Did I invite you to sit down?"

"Don't be snippy," Mason said, resting his ropy, muscled forearms on the table. "What's the matter?"

Callie thought about blowing his question off but suddenly she wanted to speak to someone with no connection to her annoying clan. "I'm arguing with my daughter." Callie sipped her coffee and eyed Mason over her mug. Because his expression, encouraging her to confide in him, scared her, she backtracked.

"She asked if you were good-looking, whether she could meet you. She's gorgeous, tall, dark-haired with the most amazing light silver-blue eyes."

"She sounds lovely but I have my heart set on dating a short, curvy blonde."

Callie looked around, wondering who he was talking about. His low, growly laugh pulled her eyes back to his amused face. "You, you twit. I want to take *you* on a date."

"I thought you were joking."

"Nope. Deadly serious."

Okay, this was weird. He seemed nice and genuine, but what was his game? "You don't want to date me, Mason."

"I've been making up my own mind for a while now and you don't get to tell me what I do and don't want." Mason's tone was soft but Callie heard the steel in his voice and, dammit, that hard note just stoked that ember of lust. Man, it had been so long since she'd felt like this around a guy, she didn't know what to say, how to act.

For the first time in thirty-plus years she wanted to kiss someone who wasn't her husband, to explore another man's body. The problem was, while he was a fine specimen for his age, she was not. Her boobs sagged, she had a muffin top and lumpy thighs. Despite her wish for sex, a one-night stand, that was more hope than expectation. And if she found the courage to expose her very flawed body to a new man, he wouldn't have the lean, muscled body of a competitive swimmer.

Mason made her feel insecure and, worse, old. There were, after all, ten years between them and, God, what a difference ten years could make. Age, the shape their bodies were in, and then there was the difference in their financial situations.

She was, not to exaggerate, filthy rich. Mason, she'd heard, was not. Did he know how wealthy she was? Was he looking for a, *ugh*, sugar mommy? What was his angle?

"Tell me about your daughter," Mason said, leaning back in his chair.

Yeah, good plan. When he heard about her family

he'd go running for the hills. "Which one? I have two by blood, one by love. I also have four sons, one by blood."

Mason blinked, ran his hand over his face and Callie laughed at his surprise. "Do you have kids?"

"Two teenage boys, fifteen and seventeen."

"My youngest, Ben, is twenty-eight," Callie said, deliberately highlighting the differences in their ages again.

"You old crone." Mason sighed, stood up and pushed his chair into the table. He placed one hand on the table, one on the back of her chair, and caged her in. His determined blue eyes drilled into hers. "You can keep fighting this, Callie, but you and I are going on a date."

The Ping-Pong ball in her throat swelled and the air left the room. He was so close that Callie could see a small scar on his upper lip, taste his sweet, coffee-flavored breath.

"And while I'm here, I might as well tell you that you and I are also going to get naked. At some point, I'm going to make you mine."

Callie was annoyed when tears burned, furious when her heart rate accelerated. "I'm not… I can't… I'm not ready."

Mason's steady expression didn't change. "I didn't say it was going to be today, Callie. But one day you will be ready and—" he lifted his hands to mimic an explosion "—boom."

Boom. Really? Callie blinked away her tears and straightened her spine. "Seriously? Does that work on other women?"

"Dunno, since you're the only one I've ever said it to." Mason bent down to drop a kiss into her hair. "Start getting used to the idea, Cal. Oh, and butt out of your kids' lives. At twenty-eight and older, they can make their own decisions."

Callie scowled at his bare back as he walked away from her. Really! Who was he to tell her how to interact with her children? And how dare he tell her that he was going to take her to bed? Did he really think that he could make a statement like that and she'd roll over and whimper her delight? He was an arrogant know-it-all with the confidence of a Hollywood A-lister.

But he also, she noticed, had a very fine butt. A butt she wouldn't mind feeling under her hands.

Noah…

Noah would've preferred to meet with Paris Barrow at her office—did the multidivorced, once-widowed socialite have an office?—but Paris insisted on meeting for a drink at April, a Charles Street bar. Hopefully, since it was late afternoon, the bar would be quiet and he could pin Paris down to some specifics with regard to the design of her yacht. Engine capacity, size, whether she wanted a monohull or a catamaran. He had to have some place to start. Oh, and getting her to sign a damn contract would be nice—at least he would be getting paid for the work he was doing.

But Paris, he decided after couple of frustrating conversations, had the attention span of a gnat…

Noah pushed his way into the bar. Another slick bar in another rich city; he'd seen many of them over the years. Looking around, he saw that his client had yet to arrive, and after ordering a beer, he slid onto a banquette, dropping his folder on the bench beside him.

It was his second full day back in Boston and, in some ways it felt like he'd never left. After being kicked out of the Brogan house by his favorite pain in the ass, he spent last night on the *Resilience* and his brothers and Levi had each brought a six-pack. They'd steadily made their way through the beers while sitting on the teak deck, their legs dangling off the side of the yacht. No one had mentioned his abrupt departure from the house and he was glad. The last thing he wanted to discuss was Jules and the past.

Noah murmured his thanks when the waitress put his beer in front of him. Taking a sip, he wished he could make the memory of Jules standing in the bathroom, looking dazed and turned on, disappear as easily as he did this beer. He'd heard the door open and turned and there she was, shirtless in the bathroom, a wet dream fantasy in full Technicolor. Her hair was around her shoulders, her slim body curvier than before, her surprisingly plump breasts covered by a pale pink lace bra. He'd immediately noticed the darker pink of her pert nipples and her flushed skin.

Then he'd made the mistake of meeting her eyes.

Noah shifted in his chair, his junk swelling at the memory. Emotions had slid in and out of her eyes; there was surprise and shock, and it was obvious that nobody had told her that he was back in town. But those emotions quickly died and he'd caught the hint of hurt before appreciation—and, yeah, flat-out furious lust—took over. Her eyes had traced his body and he knew exactly what she was thinking, because, God, he'd been thinking it, too.

He wanted her…his hands on her long, slim body, his mouth on her lips, her skin, on her secret, make-her-scream places. Whatever they started with that one kiss so long ago hadn't died. It had been slumbering for the past ten years.

Well, it was back, wide-awake and roaring and clawing…

The impulse to kiss her, to taste her again had been overwhelming, so he had. And it was as good—no, freakin' spectacular—as he thought it could be. He'd thought about dragging her back into the shower, stripping her under the water and taking her up against the tile wall. He still wanted to do that more than he wanted to breathe.

He was so screwed…

"Noah? Noah?"

Noah jerked himself out of his reverie and looked up into Paris's merry blue eyes, her face devoid of lines. Standing up—hoping he wouldn't embarrass himself—he took her outstretched hand. She looked damn good for someone in her sixties, thanks to the marvel of modern plastic surgery.

Paris sat down opposite him and put her designer bag on the table. She ordered a martini, and after the smallest of small talk, she leaned back against the banquette, eyeing him. "So, I understand that you were once engaged to Morgan Blake."

Oh, Jesus. Noah kept his face blank and waited for her to continue. "I told her that you were designing a yacht for me—"

"Well, technically I'm not. Yet," Noah clarified. "You haven't signed the contract, nor have you paid me my deposit, so right now we're still negotiating."

Paris wrinkled her nose before opening her bag and pulling out a leather case. She flipped it open and Noah saw that it was a checkbook. Paris found a pen and lifted her eyebrows. Noah gave her the figure, his heart racing as she wrote out the check. Taking it, he tucked it into his shirt pocket before withdrawing a contract from his folder. Paris signed it with a flourish and tossed her gold pen onto the table. One payment down and he'd receive the bulk of the money when she approved his final design. "Now, can we talk about Morgan?"

"No."

Paris pouted. "Why not?"

"Because we need to talk about hulls and engines and square feet and water displacement. I'm designing the yacht, but I do need some input from you," Noah said, his voice calm but firm.

Paris looked bored. "Just design me a fantastic yacht within the budget I gave you. I hear that you are ridiculously talented and wonderfully creative. Design me a vessel that will make people drool. I don't want to be bothered by the details."

The perfect scenario, Noah thought, pleased. There was nothing better than getting a green light to do what he wanted. He just hoped that Paris wouldn't change her mind down the track and morph into a nitpicking, demanding, micromanaging client. But if she did, he would handle her.

Noah handed Paris her copy of the contract, wincing when she folded it into an uneven square and shoved it into the side pocket of her bag. She drained her martini and signaled the waitress for another. "So, about Morgan."

God. Really? "Paris, I don't feel comfortable discussing this with you. You're my client."

Paris waved his measured words away. "Oh, please! I'm an absolute romantic and a terrible meddler. I nose around in everyone's business. You'll get used to it."

He most definitely would not. "There is no Morgan, Paris. That ended a long, long time ago."

"Oh, I got the impression she'd like to pick up where you left off."

Okay, it was way past time to shut this down. "Yeah, my girlfriend might object to that."

Paris's eyes gleamed with interest. "You have a girlfriend? Who is she?"

He could've mentioned Jenna in Cape Town or Yolande in London, who were both beautiful and accomplished good friends he occasionally slept with. But another name popped out of his mouth, thanks, he was sure, to a hot encounter in a bathroom yesterday morning. "Jules Brogan."

Paris's eyes widened with delight. "I know Jules. She decorated my vacation house in Hyannis Port."

Oh, crap! Crap, crap, crap.

"She was named Boston's Most Exciting Interior Designer a few months back."

She was? Why had he not heard about that? Probably the same reason the family hadn't told Jules about his return. They didn't discuss either of them ever.

"She's your girlfriend?"

"We've known each other for a long time." That, at least, was the truth.

Paris's pink mouth widened into a huge smile. "She can do the interior decoration for my yacht. Aren't you supposed to give me an idea of the interior when you present the final design?"

Oh, hell, he didn't like this. At all. "Yes. But I have my team of decorators I normally work with in London," Noah stated, wondering how this conversation had veered so off track. Oh, right, maybe because he *lied*?

"I want Jules," Paris said, looking stubborn. Her face hardened and Noah caught a glimpse of a woman who always got what she wanted. "Do not make me tear up that contract and ask for my check back, Noah."

Je-sus. Noah rubbed the back of his neck. She would do exactly as she said. Paris wanted what she wanted and expected to get it. *No* did not feature in her vocabulary.

Noah leaned back, sighed and eyed his pain-in-the-ass client. "You're going to be a handful, aren't you?" he asked, resigned.

Paris's expression lightened. "Oh, honey, you have no idea. So, what should I tell Morgan?"

Noah groaned and ordered a double whiskey.

Jules...

Jules heard the muted sound coming from her phone and, without looking at the screen, silenced the alert. Eight thirty in the morning and today was, Jules squinted at the bottom right corner of her computer, Thursday. The only way to stop thinking about Noah, and his wet, naked, ripped body, and the fact that he was back in her orbit, was to go back to work. Instead of taking the break she needed, she slid right back into sixteen-hour days and creating long and detailed schedules so that nothing slipped through the cracks.

Jules moved her mouse and today's to-do list appeared on her monitor.

The reminder of her 9:00 a.m. meeting with the girls was followed by a list of her appointments with clients, suppliers and craftspeople. Her last appointment was at five thirty, and then she had to hustle to make her appointment with her beautician, Dana, for an eyebrow shape and a bikini wax. She was not going to dwell on the fact that the bikini wax was a last-minute request.

It had nothing to do with looking good for a brown-eyed blond.

You keep telling yourself that, sweet pea.

Jules reached for her cup of now-cold coffee and pulled a face when the icy liquid hit the back of her throat. Yuck. Resisting the urge to wipe her tongue on the sleeve of her white button-down shirt, she pushed back her chair. Her phone released the discreet trill of an incoming call and Jules frowned down at the screen, not recognizing the number. As early as it was, she couldn't ignore the call; too many of her clients and suppliers had this number and she needed to be available to anybody at any time.

"Jules."

She recognized his voice instantly, the way he said her name, the familiar tone sliding over her skin. "Noah."

There had been a time when she'd laugh with excitement to get a call from him, when her heart would swell from just hearing his voice. But those were childish reactions and she was no longer the child who'd hero-worshipped Noah, or the teenager who'd thought the sun rose and set with him. He was no longer her best friend, the person she could say anything to, the one person who seemed to get her on a deeper level than even her twin did.

"What do you want, Lockwood?"

"We need to talk."

"Exactly what I said to you ten years ago," Jules said, wincing at the bitterness in her voice. After their kiss, he'd avoided her, ducked her calls. She hadn't suspected he was leaving until he came by her mom's house one evening to say goodbye. The kiss was never mentioned. When she asked to speak to him privately he'd refused, explaining that he didn't have time, that there was nothing to discuss. He and Morgan were still engaged. He was dropping out of college. He was going sailing. He didn't know how often he would be in contact.

Please don't worry about him. He'd be fine.

She'd been so damn happy to receive his first email, had soaked up his news, happy to know that he was safe and leading the race. He'd spoken about the brilliant sunsets, a pod of southern right whales, a squall they'd encountered that day, the lack of winds the next. Reading his words made her feel like they were connected again, that their relationship could be salvaged...

Then she noticed the email was sent to a group and that her mom, her siblings, his siblings, plus a few of his college buds, received the same message. Jules never received a personalized email, nor did she receive one of his infrequent calls back home. She'd been relegated to the periphery of his life and it stung like a band of fire ants walking over her skin. She still didn't understand how someone who meant everything to her had vanished like he was never part of her life at all.

"There's nothing to say, Noah. Too much water under the hull and all that. We're adults. We can be civil in company, but let's not try and resurrect something that is very definitely over."

"Oh, it's not over, Jules. We're just starting a new chapter of a yet-unwritten book," Noah replied softly. Then his voice strengthened and turned businesslike. "I do need to talk to you—I need to hire you."

Jules dropped her phone, stared at the screen and

shook her head. "Yeah, that's not going to happen. Speaking of work, I'm late for a meeting."

"Do not hang up on me, Ju—"

Jules pressed the red phone icon on her screen and tossed the device onto her messy desk. Work with him? Seriously? Not in this lifetime.

The display room of Winston and Brogan doubled as a conference room, and most mornings Jules, Darby and DJ started their day with a touch-base meeting, drinking their coffee as the early-morning Charles Street pedestrians passed by their enormous window. Jules sat down on a porcelain-blue-and-white-striped chair and thought that it was time to redesign their showroom. It was small, but it was the first impression clients received when they walked through the door, and it was time for something new, fresh.

"Creams or blush or jewel colors?" Jules threw the question into the silence before taking a sip of her caramel latte.

Darby didn't look up from her phone. "Jewel colors. Let's make this place pop."

"Whatever you two think is best," DJ replied, as she always did. Jules smiled, her friend was a whiz with money but, unlike her and Darby, she didn't have a creative bone in her body. They made an effective team. Darby designed buildings. Jules decorated them, and DJ managed their money.

The fact that they worked so well together was the main reason their full house design firm was one of the best in the city. Oh, they fought… They'd known each other all of their lives and they knew exactly what buttons to push to get a nuclear reaction. But they never fought dirty and none of them held grudges. Well, she would if they allowed her to, which they never did.

Darby crossed her legs and Jules admired the spiky heel dangling off her foot. The shoe was a perfect shade of nude with a heart-shaped peep toe. So, she'd be borrowing those soon. Hell, they'd shared the same womb, sharing clothes was a given.

"Tina Harper, she was at college with us, is pregnant. Four months." Darby looked up from her cell and Jules noticed that her smile was forced. Her heart contracted, knowing that under that brave face her sister ached for what could not be. When they were teenagers, Darby was told that, thanks to chronic endometriosis, the chances of her conceiving a child were slim to none. Closer to none… It was her greatest wish to be a mama, with or without a man. And the way their love lives were progressing, it would probably be without one.

"Didn't she date Ben?" DJ asked.

Darby shrugged. "God, I don't know. At one point, Ben had a revolving door to his bedroom."

"Ben still has a revolving door to his bedroom," Jules pointed out, thinking of the youngest Lockwood brother. He was probably the best-looking of the three gorgeous Lockwood boys and he was never short of a date or five. She could say the same for her brother, Levi, and Eli and, she assumed, Noah.

Noah. Jules sucked her bottom lip between her teeth.

As always, just thinking his name dropped her stomach to the floor, caused her heart to bounce off her rib cage. Remembering their half-naked kiss threatened to stop her heart altogether.

"So, how does it feel having Noah back?" DJ asked.

"He's back in your life, not mine," Jules replied, trying to sound casual.

She'd been interrogated by every member of her family so they could find out what had caused the cold war between her and Noah. Her stock answer, "We just drifted apart," resulted in rolling eyes and disbelieving snorts but she never elaborated. They periodically still asked her for an explanation. She knew Noah was staying mum because a) Noah wasn't the type to dish, and b) if he had, then the news would've spread like wildfire. The Brogan/Lockwood clan was not known for discretion. Or keeping good gossip to themselves.

Sometimes she was tempted to tell them that she and Noah had shared some blisteringly hot kisses just to see the expression on their faces. But then the questions would follow... Why hadn't they explored that attraction? Why couldn't they get past it?

It was a question that, when she allowed it to, kept her up at night. Why hadn't they dealt with the situation, addressed the belly dancing elephant in the room?

Ah, maybe it was because, shortly after kissing her ten years back, Noah flew Morgan to Vegas to, she assumed, celebrate their engagement. Their kiss, him dropping out of college, his engagement, him turning pro... He'd made every decision without asking her opinion. Okay, she understood that he wasn't obliged to check in with her but she had run everything past him and he did talk to her about his dreams, his plans. That Christmas season, Noah had clammed up and it felt like twenty-plus years of friendship had meant nothing to him…

That he and Morgan never married wasn't a surprise, nor was it a consolation. He'd wasted two years of his time, his money and attention on Morgan, but it was his time and money to waste. Still, Jules couldn't help feeling that his engagement was a big "up yours" to their newly discovered attraction. His lack of communication, blasé explanations and his lack of effort to maintain their friendship had severed their connection. Because she would never be able to fully trust him again, they could never be friends again.

And being lovers was out of the question. That required an even deeper level of trust she was incapable of feeling.

"Did you date anyone in California?" Darby asked her, pulling her attention off the past.

She had actually. "Mmm."

"Really? And…?" Darby asked, intrigued.

"Two dates and I called it quits. Since we live on opposite sides of the country, there was no point."

She always gave guys two dates to make an impression before she moved on, thinking that dating was stressful and who got anything right the first date? If they had potential, she extended the period, making sure that hands and mouths stayed out of the equation. Not many made it to twelve weeks and most of those didn't pass her was-he-a-better-kisser-than-Noah? test. Actually, none of them were better kissers, but the two who came close made it into her bed. One lasted another few weeks; the other went back to his ex-girlfriend.

She hadn't had a relationship that went beyond four months since college…and at nearly thirty she'd only had three lovers. How sad was that?

Yet, she continued to date, thinking that one day she'd find someone who made her forget about that nuclear hot kiss on a snowy evening so damn long ago. She had to find someone. There was no way she'd allow her best sexual memory to be of Noah Lockwood…ten years or four days ago.

"Maybe I should go back on Tinder," Jules mused, mostly to herself. But at the thought, her heart backed into the corner of her chest, comprehensively horrified. She didn't blame it, meeting guys on the internet was a crappy way to find love. Or to find a date with a reasonably normal man.

"Oh, come on," DJ retorted, calling her bluff. "Psychos, weirdos and losers. You don't need any of that."

"Says the girl who has sex on a semiregular basis," Jules murmured. Since college, DJ had an on-off relationship with Matt, a human rights lawyer, who dropped in and out of her life. It was all about convenience, DJ blithely informed them, and about great sex with a guy she liked and respected.

Jules wanted one of those.

"Please stay off the net, Jules," Darby begged. "You are a magnet for crazies."

Jules couldn't argue the point. All she wanted was to meet guys like her brother and Eli and Ben. Despite their grasshopper mentality when it came to women, the three of them—even, dammit, Noah—were interesting, smart, driven and successful men. They were honest and trustworthy—well, three out of four were—and she wanted a man like them and her dad. Was she asking too much? Were her brother and her friends the last good men left in Boston? And if she found that elusive man, would she ever be able to trust him not to hurt her long enough for her to fall in love? Or would her fear send her running?

DJ gently kicked her shin with the toe of her shoe and Jules blinked, lifting a shoulder at DJ's scowl. "What?"

"Why don't you take a break from dating for a while, Jules? You've been scraping the barrel lately. Whatever you are looking for, you're not finding."

Darby tipped her head. "What *are* you looking for?"

Jules stared out of the window. *I'm looking for a guy who makes me feel as alive as I do when Noah kisses me. I'm looking for a guy who will make me stop thinking about him, stop missing him, who will fill the hole he left in my life. I'm looking for someone who will make me feel the same way I did during that bold, bright moment the other day. Noah can't be the only man who can make me feel intensely alive... That would be cruel. No, there is someone else out there. There has to be...*

Noah was the only man who made her explore the

outer edges of love and despair, attraction and loathing. Kissing Noah made her feel sexy and feminine and powerful beyond measure. But his actions when they were younger made her feel insignificant and irrelevant. He'd hurtled her from nirvana into a hell she hadn't been prepared for.

He'd dismissed her opinions, ignored her counsel, and those actions she could, maybe, forgive. But she'd never forgive him for destroying their friendship, for flicking her out of his life like she was a piece of filthy gum stuck to his shoe.

DJ clapped her hands, signaling that she was moving into work mode. Jules forced herself to think business. She had designs to draw up for a revamp to a historic bed-and-breakfast, craftspeople to meet to finalize the furnishings for a bar in Back Bay. Maybe she should stop dating for a while and immerse herself in work. They had enough of it to keep them all busy for months, if not years.

"Profit and loss, expense reports... I need your receipts," DJ said, and Jules wrinkled her nose. "I need the cost estimates on the Duncan job."

"Ack," Jules said. She loved designing but hated the paperwork it generated. "Deadline?"

"Yesterday."

"Hard-ass," Jules muttered.

"I am," DJ replied, not at all insulted. "That's why we are in the black, darling. It's all me."

Darby and Jules laughed, knowing that DJ was joking. They were a team and each of them was an essential cog in the wheel. As always, they were stronger together.

Darby looked at her watch and stood up, nearly six feet of tall grace. Jules looked out of the window and lifted her hand to wave at Dani, the personal assistant they shared, Merry, their shop floor assistant and their two interns.

Her smiled faded when she saw who was standing behind them, six feet four inches of muscle wearing chinos, a blue oxford shirt and a darker blue jacket. His wavy hair was cut short and, like always, he was days beyond shaving that dark blond scruff off his face.

Through the display window, his eyes met hers and her stomach contracted, her heart flip-flopped and all the moisture in her mouth disappeared.

It seemed that Noah did indeed intend to talk.

Three

Jules...

Jules shoved her hands under her thighs and tingles ran up and down her spinal column. Darby and DJ turned in their seats to see who'd captured her attention and immediately jumped to their feet, their beautiful faces showing their delight at seeing him. Noah was, always had been, one of their favorite people.

Kisses and hugs were exchanged and while her sisters—one by blood and the other of the heart—and Noah did a quick catch-up, Jules allowed her eyes the rare pleasure to roam. Tall, broad, blond, hot...all the adjectives had been used in various ways to describe him, and Noah was all of those things. But Jules, because she'd once known him so well, could look beneath the hot, sexy veneer.

There were fine lines around those startling eyes and a tiny frown pulled his thick sandy brows together. He was smiling but it wasn't the open, sunny smile from their childhoods, the one that could knock out nuclear reactors with one blinding flash. The muscles in his neck were tense and under the blond scruff, his jaw was rock hard.

Noah was not a happy camper.

Noah stepped away from Darby and DJ and their eyes met, the power of a thousand unsaid words flowing between them. Noah pushed back his navy jacket and jammed his hands into the pockets of his stone-colored pants, rocking on his feet. His eyes left hers, dropped to her mouth, down to her chest, over her hips and slowly meandered their way back up. Every inch he covered sent heat and lust coursing through her system, reminding her with crystal clear certainty what being held by him, kissed by him was like. Suddenly, she was eighteen again and willing to follow him wherever he led…

The thought annoyed her, so her voice was clipped when she finally remembered how to use her tongue. "What are you doing here, Noah?"

Noah pulled his hands from his pockets to cross his arms and his eyes turned frosty. "Nice to see you, too, Jules."

Darby, sensing trouble, jumped into the conversation. "Do you have time for coffee, Noah?"

Noah shook his head. "Thanks, hon, but no."

Jules linked her shaking hands around one knee. "Why are you here, Noah?"

"Business," Noah replied. He held out his hand and jerked his head to the spiral staircase that led up to the second floor, the boardroom and their personal offices. "You and I need to talk."

Jules didn't trust herself to touch him—he was too big and too male and too damn attractive. She didn't trust herself not to throw herself into his arms and slap her mouth against his, so she ignored his hand and slowly stood up. After taking a moment to brush nonexistent lint off her linen pants, and to get her raging hormones under some sort of order, she darted a look at Darby and then DJ, and they both looked as puzzled as she did. "Okay. I have some time before my conference call in thirty minutes."

She didn't have a call, but if dealing with Noah became too overwhelming, she wanted an out. Walking to the spiral staircase, she gestured for Noah to follow her. As they made their way up the stairs she could smell his subtle, sexy cologne, could feel his heat.

She was two steps ahead of him. If she turned around, right at that moment, they would be the same height and their mouths would be perfectly aligned. She could look straight into those deep, dark eyes and lose herself, feel his mouth soften under hers, find out whether his short beard was as soft as it looked, whether the cords of his neck, revealed by the open collar of his button-down shirt, were as hard as they looked.

She hadn't touched him long enough the other morning, and if she turned around, she wouldn't have to wonder...

Jules gave herself a mental head slap and carried on walking. How could they go from friends who'd never so much as thought of each other in that way to two people who wanted to inhale each other? And, dammit, how could she suddenly be this person who wanted to rip his clothes off and lick him from top to toe?

Jules groaned silently as she hit the top step and turned right to head for her corner office. Giving herself another mental slap, she reminded herself that she would rather die than give Noah the smallest hint that he still affected her, that she'd spent far too much time lately remembering him naked, imagining his hands on either side of her head, lowering himself so that the tip of his...

Oh, dear God, Brogan! Jules curled her arm across her waist and pinched her side, swallowing her hiss of pain. *Get a grip! Now!*

At her office door, Jules sucked in a breath and stepped inside her messy space.

Making a beeline for the chair behind her desk— she needed a barrier of wood and steel between her and Lockwood—she gestured him to take the sole visitor's chair opposite her. Steeling herself, she met his eyes and opened her hands. "So, business. What's up?"

Noah...

Noah sat down in the visitor's chair and placed his ankle on his knee, thinking that Jules's eyes were the color of a perfect early morning breaking over a calm sea. Light, a curious combination of blue and gray and silver. Looking into her eyes took him back to those perfect mornings of possibility, to being on the sea, where freedom was wind in the sails and the sun on his face.

If the dark hair and light eyes combo wasn't enough to have his brain stuttering, then God added a body that was long, slim and perfectly curved and, as he remembered, fragrant and so damn soft to the touch. Being this close to her, inhaling the light floral scent of her perfume, in the messy, colorful space filled with fabric swatches and sketches, magazines and bolts of fabric, Noah's lungs collapsed from a lack of air.

The urge to run was strong, away from her and the memories she yanked to the surface.

A decade ago there had been reasons to distance himself from Jules, including that clause written into his sponsorship deal with Wind and Solar. As a new year bloomed he'd grasped that his friend was no longer a child or a girl but a woman who he was very attracted to. They'd kissed and he knew they could never be lovers because they were such good friends. Two seconds later the thought had hit him that they could never be friends because they had the potential to be amazing lovers.

Walking away from her, shivering, into the falling snow, he knew something fundamental had shifted inside him and that there was only one thing he was sure of: their friendship would never be the same again.

Now and then, whether it was monster waves or his

mom's death or Ethan morphing from a loving father into a money-grabbing bastard, Noah faced life head-on with his chin and fists raised. He had the ability to see situations clearly, to not get bogged down in the emotion of a life event. As tempted as he'd been to say to hell with everyone and fall into the romance of the moment—best friends kissing and being blown away by it!—he'd been smart enough to know that decision would come back to bite him in the ass.

Even if he'd been able to push aside his other problems back then—no money for the legal fights and his fake engagement to Morgan—he knew he was standing in a bucket on an angry sea. They couldn't be friends or lovers or anything in between. Her siblings were his and vice versa. They shared two dozen or more mutual friends and her parents were two of his favorite people. He and Levi had been talking about going into business together since they were in their early teens. He and Jules had been—were still—tied together by many silken cords, and if they changed the parameters of their relationship and it went south, those cords would be shredded.

If Jules hurt him, his brothers would jump to his defense despite the fact that they adored Jules; she was their sister from another mother. If he hurt Jules, her family would haul him over the coals… Either way, the dynamic of their blended family would be changed forever and he would not be responsible for that.

He could not relinquish the little that was left of the Lockwood legacy because of one kiss, a fantasy moment. He had to save the boatyard and the marina, and now the estate, if not for him, then for his two brothers. He owed it to his mom to keep Ethan's grubby, money-grabbing paws from what was hers and, morally, theirs.

"Are you just going to sit there in silence, or do I have to guess why you are here?"

Jules's snippy voice pulled him out of the past and Noah blinked before running his hand over his face. Right. He did, actually, have a valid, business-related reason to be there.

"Congratulations on your award as the best designer in the city, Ju," Noah said. Despite his frustration with the situation, he was extraordinarily proud of her. He'd always known she was an incredibly talented designer. But he hadn't expected her and DJ and Darby to create such a successful and dynamic business in so short of a time. People said that his level of success was meteoric, he had nothing on Jules and her friends. From concept to kudos in four years, they were a phenomenal and formidable team.

"Thank you," Jules replied, her voice cool. She rolled her finger, impatient.

Right, time to sink or swim. Noah preferred to, well, sail. "I have a job for you."

Jules's small smile didn't reach her eyes. "Not interested. I'm booked solid for months."

Yeah, he'd expected that. "I'm designing a super-yacht, a bit of a departure from the racing yachts I've developed my reputation on. My client is pretty adamant that she wants you to design the interiors."

"As interesting as that project would be, I can't take on another client, Noah. It's just not possible."

Jules leaned back in her chair and crossed her legs. Her eyes were now a cool gray and Noah knew she was enjoying having him at her mercy, being able to say no. Jules was taking her revenge on him for walking out of her life and, yeah, he got it, he'd hurt her. But the hell of it was that he needed her. He needed her now more than he ever had before.

Ignoring his need to save Lockwood Estate, his reputation depended on him persuading her to say yes. Noah opened his mouth to explain, to tell her how much rested on him gaining her help and cooperation but his phone rang, stopping him in his tracks. Grateful for the reprieve, he pulled his phone out of the inside pocket of his jacket and glanced down at the screen. A once-familiar number popped up on his screen.

The thought that there was no way she'd still have the same phone number as so long ago jumped into his mind. Then he remembered that he'd had the same number all of his life.

But why would Morgan be phoning him? Confused and shocked, he shook his head and tucked his phone, the call unanswered, back into his jacket pocket. He had nothing to say to his ex and never would.

"So, as fun as this nonconversation has been, I need to get back to work," Jules said, standing up and gesturing to the door.

Noah cursed softly and pushed an irritated hand

through his hair. "Ju, we need to talk. At least, I need to talk—"

Jules placed both hands on the desk and glared at him, her eyes laser cold. "No, Noah, we really don't! You don't get to walk into my office demanding my time when you walked out of my life years ago, tossing our friendship without a word of explanation. How dare you think you can demand that I work for you when you treated me like I was nothing?"

Jules shook her head, her eyes glistening with unshed tears. "I mourned you. I mourned what we had. You abandoned me, Noah. You walked away from me and our friendship like it was nothing, like I was nothing." Jules circled her desk, headed toward the door and yanked it open. She rested her forehead on the door frame, and for the first time Noah realized how much he'd hurt her. Suddenly, his heart was under the spiky heel of her shoe.

No one knew, nobody had the faintest idea, how hard it was for him to leave Boston. On the surface it had been a pretty sweet deal, he'd been offered the money he needed and he had the opportunity for travel and adventure. He was twenty-three years old and the world was his playground. But underneath the jokes and the quips, his heart wept bloody tears. He was still mourning his mom, feeling helpless and angry at her death. He was gas-fire mad with Ethan for treating her like crap and lying to them.

His stability, everything he knew was in Boston: it was in the kind eyes and solid, unpushy support of

Callie and Ray, in Levi and his brothers standing at his side, not talking but being there, a solid wall between him and the world. It had been in DJ's and Darby's hugs, in their upbeat, daily text messages.

It had been everything—her smile, her understanding, her kisses, her laugh—about Jules.

Leaving meant distance, walking away from everything that made sense. It had been frickin' terrifying and, apart from burying his mom, the hardest thing he'd ever done. Sailing that tempestuous, ass-cold Southern Ocean had been child's play compared to leaving Boston. And, because he'd just barely survived leaving once, he knew he couldn't fall back into the life he had before. He wouldn't allow himself to rely on Levi's friendship, Callie's support, his brothers' wall and Jules's ability to make everything both better and brighter. Because he couldn't survive losing any of it again.

Once was ten times too many…

Jules gestured for Noah to leave. "I have a call I need to take. Clients to look after."

Noah stood up and pushed his hands through his hair. Okay, this was salvageable. He would just tell Paris that Jules wasn't available, wouldn't be for some time. This wasn't a train smash. It was business. Paris would understand that. *It was business…*

In fact, it would be better if he and Jules didn't work together. Professional wasn't something he could be around Jules.

At the door, Noah stopped in front of Jules and bent his knees to look into her spectacular eyes. He wanted to explain, to banish some of the pain he saw there. "I never meant to hurt you, Jules."

Jules looked up at him and lifted her chin, her eyes flashing defiance. "But you did, Noah. And you still haven't explained why."

He didn't do explanations. Noah sighed, dropped a quick kiss on her temple—the intoxicating scent of her filling his nose—and before his hands and mouth did something stupid, he walked away.

It was only when he reached the sidewalk that his heart started to beat normally again, when his brain regained full power.

Noah stepped off the sidewalk to hail a cab. It was a good thing Jules have didn't the time—or the inclination—to work for him; she turned his brain to mush.

Jules...

The following Saturday, Jules picked up two breakfast rolls and made her way to the marina, where she knew she could find her brother, Levi. Despite them living in the same house, it had been ages since she'd spent any time with her older brother and she was looking forward to seeing him, but she did, admittedly, have an ulterior motive. She needed him to make a steel frame for a coffee table, and Levi, or rather the newly named Lockwood-Brogan Marina, owned a welding machine.

Along with his business degree, Levi also knew how to weld and the ham-and-egg sandwich was her way to bribe him. If Levi couldn't, or wouldn't, she'd ask Eli or Ben...

All three Lockwood boys and Levi had held part-time and summer jobs at the marina, and they all knew how to use their hands; Noah's grandfather had made sure of that. As a result, she and her sisters rarely had to pay for home repairs.

Besides, the boys had frequently made their lives hell: short-sheeting their beds, hiding their dolls, scaring the crap out of them. Making them work was payback.

Jules, dressed in a pink-and-red-patterned sundress and flip-flops, walked into the blessedly cool reception area of the marina and smiled at Levi's new receptionist, Meredith. The young blonde was talking to a middle-aged couple but she smiled before lifting her chin, silently telling her that Levi was in his office. Jules nodded her thanks, walked behind the counter and down the short passage to the end office, which had a spectacular view of the marina. Levi, dark-haired and blue-eyed, had his feet up on his desk and his tablet on his knees.

"Playing 'Angry Birds'?" Jules asked, tossing his sandwich into his lap.

"You know me too well." Levi placed his tablet on his messy desk and lifted the packet to his nose. He narrowed his eyes at Jules. "Ham and egg... What do you want?"

"A frame to be welded."

Levi unwrapped his sandwich, and after taking a bite, chewing and swallowing, he shook his head. "Eli is better at welding than me. Or, better yet, he can send one of his welders from the shipyard to do it."

"But that will take forever."

Jules perched on the edge of his desk, leaving her sandwich in front of him. If necessary, she'd bribe him with the second sandwich to get her frame welded today. She batted her eyelashes at him, knowing that he loved to be adored. "Please, Lee? You have a welding machine and you're—" she gestured to his tablet "—obviously not busy. The steel bars are already in your workshop at home."

Levi glared at her. "For your information, I was going over our financials."

The note of worry in his voice caught Jules's attention. "Everything okay?"

Levi was slow to respond, but when he did, his face carried no hint of his normal good humor. "Noah and I recently bought a majority share of the marina on the waterfront and are in the process of updating the facilities. We're asset rich and cash flow tight at the moment."

"But you're okay?"

Levi nodded. "I am. The businesses are. I'm not so sure about Noah. He's seriously stressed and I know it's money related. Did you know that he wants to buy the Lockwood Country Club Estate off Ethan?"

Jules frowned, confused. "Buy it? Why would he buy it since the Lockwood Trust owns it?"

"But Ethan owns the Lockwood Trust, not Noah and the guys. Ethan was awarded the estate when the boys took Ethan to court. How do you not know this?"

Because she never talked to or about Noah?

"Did you not wonder why Noah was staying with us, why he's sleeping on the *Resilience* and not at Lockwood House?"

"Well, I did, but—" Jules ended her sentence with a shrug. "I knew Ethan and Noah had a falling-out but not much more than that. So, what happened?"

Levi held up a hand. "Ask Noah. If he wants you to know, he'll tell you."

Jules's mouth dropped open. "You don't know either!"

Levi shrugged. "Noah doesn't talk much. You know that."

She really did. "So, what do you know?" Okay, she was curious, she'd cop to that.

Levi pushed a hand through his dark hair. "The guys need to raise a cracking amount of cash in order to get a mortgage to buy the estate off Ethan. In order to do that Noah needs to finish the design on the yacht he's working on but his client is being difficult."

"Noah always delivers. That's what he's known for, what he does." Noah was exceptionally good at what he did and was reputed to be one of the best racing yacht designers in the world.

"Well, this client wants something that Noah can't deliver and if he doesn't deliver, he won't get paid. If he doesn't get paid, he can't buy Lockwood House and the estate."

My client is pretty adamant that she wants you to design the interiors. Her heart and stomach dropped to the floor as Jules remembered Noah's words in her office. Her firm "no" had put his project, buying his family house and land, in jeopardy. *God, Noah.*

Levi continued to speak. "The client isn't listening and Noah's project is up the creek. Without her cash, he can't buy the estate. Without the estate, he doesn't get Lockwood House. And you know how much the house means to him."

Yeah, she did. All his memories of his mom were tied up in that house, in the country club she managed and the land she loved.

Levi balled his wax paper and threw it into the wastepaper bin across the room. He eyed the second sandwich. "I'll do your welding this afternoon if you hand over that sandwich."

Instead of tossing him the second sandwich, she scooped it up and headed for the door. "Hey! Where are you going with that sandwich?"

At the door, Jules turned. "Is Noah using Grandpa Lockwood's old office and is he there?"

Levi nodded. "Should be. He works longer hours than I do." He sent her his patented I'm-hungry-feed-me look that was difficult to resist. But Jules had other plans for her sandwich, so she left his office and headed for the spiral staircase at the end of the hall, the one that would take her to the conference room and Noah's office.

"I'm not welding your frame without the sandwich!" Levi's words trailed after her.

She didn't care. She had a bigger problem to fix.

Four

Noah...

Noah, dressed in navy cargo shorts and a gray T-shirt under an open denim shirt, turned away from his architect's desk as she walked into his office without knocking. Standing in the doorway, she noticed his look of complete surprise before his face settled back into its inscrutable can't-faze-me expression.

"Jules. Good morning."

To hell with being polite, they were so far past that. "Why didn't you tell me that your project was in jeopardy?"

Noah lifted his broad shoulders in a weary shrug. "You're busy. I can't expect you to drop your other projects just because I asked. I thought my client was being unreasonable and that I could persuade her to consider other designers."

"Did you manage to do that?"

Noah tossed his pencil onto the desk and rubbed his fingers into his eye sockets. "Nope."

"So I'm it or you lose the project?"

Noah twisted his lips and finally nodded. "Basically." He lifted a hand. "Don't worry about it, Jules. I have other clients who have been begging me to design racing yachts. It's not a big deal."

Jules leaned her shoulder into the door frame. "But if you lose this project, you lose all your work and also the ability to buy back Lockwood House and everything else."

"Levi and his big mouth. I'll make a plan. If I don't buy it this time around, I'll wait until it comes back on the market and buy it then. For the first time since 1870 it'll leave Lockwood hands, but I'll get it back."

Jules saw the determination in his eyes. He would eventually take back his family's legacy but at what price? God, he'd already lost his mom and his home, was it fair that he lose this opportunity, too? Who knew when he'd get the chance to purchase Lockwood Estate again, if ever?

A management company ran the country club and estate but Jules couldn't bear the thought of another family owning and living in Beth's beloved and historic house; they might add on, rip it down, change it. No, a Lockwood deserved to live there or at the very least, the house should remain empty until one of the brothers decided he was going to move back in.

She hadn't recognized the consequences of her decision, because Noah hadn't told her, and she could kick him for that. If she'd known, she wouldn't have hesitated. This affected not only Noah but Eli and Ben, and her refusal to help felt like she was letting Bethann and her sons down. Yes, she was busy, but she could delegate work to her assistants and carve out some time for the project.

Jules walked into his office, dumped her bag onto his chair and placed the sandwich on his mostly empty desk. She couldn't eat; this was too important. But he might be hungry.

"Eat up, and when you're done, we'll go over the design brief."

Noah sent her a hard stare. "You're going to take the job?"

Jules rolled her eyes so hard that she was sure she could see her butt. "Of course I am."

"Why?" Noah demanded, his eyes wary.

"Because, as annoying as you are, you and that house are a part of my family, and family steps up when there's a problem. You need this job to be able to buy that house, and to raise the money to do that, you need me. There's no way that I am going to be responsible for the estate passing out of Lockwood hands. Bethann might start haunting me."

"It's a strong possibility and something I'm also worried about."

Noah looked down and, judging by the way his shoulders dropped, Jules knew he was trying to hide his relief. He hated anyone to see that he was worried, to think that he was weak. He liked the world to think that he was a tough-guy sailor, one who took enormous risks with aplomb, conquered high waves with a whoop and a yell, and he liked them to think that he did it with ease. Jules was the only person, apart from maybe her parents, who'd glimpsed the turmoil roiling inside of him.

But Jules, as always, saw more than she should and, standing in his office, in front of this delicious-looking man, she sensed the tension seeping from him, could taste his relief. And suddenly, weirdly, she wanted to put her arms around his waist, lay her head on his chest and tell him that it would be all right. That they would be all right. But, as much as she wanted to do that, she couldn't.

She'd trusted Noah once, trusted him with her deepest fears and feelings, her innermost thoughts. But he'd dismissed her, abandoned their friendship and ignored her.

No, she couldn't allow herself to be seduced by memories, to fall back into that space where the world was a brighter, better place with Noah in it. He was her client, sort of, and she had a job to do. This would be business and only business. She could never regain what was lost.

She'd work with Noah, give him her best effort but she'd never ever trust him again.

"Thanks, Jules. But before you accept, there's something else you should know."

That didn't sound good… Noah pulled in a deep breath before dropping his conversational grenade. "My client thinks that we're dating."

"Sorry?"

"She thinks you are my girlfriend, lover… Call it what you will."

Jules stared at him, her insides feeling like they were on a roller-coaster ride. His girlfriend? Why would his client think that? And why did the idea of being with Noah, tall, built and ripped, send shivers of…well, lust, up and back down her spine? What was wrong with her?

And, oh, Lord, being alone with him was an exercise in restraint. Yeah, she was still angry that he'd walked out on her, that he ignored her for years—no, she wasn't angry, she was hurt—but, worse than that, she was on fire, inside and out. Jules licked her lips and then swallowed, trying to get some moisture back into her mouth. Between her legs, an ancient drumbeat thrummed and her nipples pushed against the fabric of her pretty lace bra.

Just because Noah mentioned that someone thought that they were lovers. Ridiculous to the nth degree.

Jules dropped her eyes from his chest, allowed them to bounce off his muscled thighs before staring at the black and brown slate tiles that covered his office floor. She shouldn't be thinking about how attractive she found him. She had bigger problems than that to deal with. Like the fact that his client thought they were dating.

Uh…why would their client think they were dating?

Jules's eyes darted up to meet his, her eyebrows rising. "Want to explain how I went from being your designer to your girlfriend?"

Noah looked equally frustrated. "She was trying to set me up with…someone, so I said that I have a girlfriend. She asked who she was, your name was the first name that popped into my head."

Really? Surely he had a dozen names he could've thrown at his client. Noah was a good-looking, sexy, moderately famous and very successful guy. He had to have an encyclopedia-size black book of eligible candidates suitable to be his arm candy, so why did her name leave his lips?

"Because this is Boston, which is in some ways a ludicrously small town, she recognized your name and got all excited, insisting that she knew you and your work and that she wanted no one else to design her interiors."

Well, she'd made an impression on someone. A rich someone who had the money to buy a phenomenally expensive yacht. "As long as your client isn't Paris Barrow. I'm prepared to work with anyone but her."

Noah closed his eyes and Jules groaned her dismay. No! Why was the universe torturing her? She not only had to work with her oldest friend who now made all her hormones jump, but she also had to work with the client from hell? Paris wasn't mean but she found it hard to make a decision and stick to it. One day it was pastels, the next earth tones, a week later it was the colors of the Mediterranean. Wood, then steel, then ceramic, then a combination of all three.

Paris lived in her own world, surrounded by people whose mission in life was to make her happy. What Paris wanted, Paris got. Even if that meant changing her mind a hundred times.

She was a deliciously sweet, generous nightmare of epic proportions.

And, worse than that, she was incredibly nosy and horribly romantic. Married multiple times, widowed once, each and every one of her husbands was the love of her life. She was, so Jules heard, on the lookout for husband number six. Paris wouldn't be content with the idea of her and Noah just dating. Before she could blink twice, Paris would have them engaged and booking a church.

Jules tossed up her hands. "Uh-uh, no way. Not Paris Barrow, you're on your own."

Noah smiled, flashing white teeth. "Chicken," he murmured.

Jules hopped off her stool and slapped her hands on her hips. "She's like a walking, talking dating show! Everyone around her drops like flies when she comes into their lives."

Noah lifted an eyebrow. "Dead?"

Jules waved her hands to dismiss his words. "No! They fall in love, get married, get engaged. She's, again, a walking, talking bottle of fairy dust! And you told her that we're dating?"

"No, I told her that you were my girlfriend. One step up," Noah replied, very unhelpfully.

"Oh, God. She's going to harass us about the fact that we're not engaged, not married. Paris is a staunch proponent of buying the cow before you drink the milk."

Noah's low laugh danced over her skin. "I think you're making too big a deal about this, Ju. We pretend to be lovers, she harasses us a little, we resist. It's all good."

Jules sent him a dark look. "You have no idea what you're dealing with."

Noah folded his arms and his biceps pulled the fabric of his shirt tighter. Jules sighed, he had the sexiest arms she'd ever seen. Bar none. Noah's brown eyes turned serious. "Is our dating going to be a problem for you?"

For some reason Jules wanted to reassure him that there wasn't anybody in her life who caught her interest. Except him. Since he'd walked back into her office, into her life, she couldn't stop thinking about him, wondering how he tasted, whether his strength would be a counter to her softness, whether they'd be the perfect fit she imagined.

More than the physical attraction, there was a part of her that wished she could go back, to reexplore their closeness, to plumb his mind. She'd enjoyed the way he thought, his analytical brain, the tenderness beneath the suit of armor he wore. The combination of attraction and friendship was lethal. It could lead to more than she was ready for, for much more than she could deal with. No, she could not go back to what they had;

it was dead. She couldn't risk having Noah in her life again and losing him.

It had nearly broken her once. There was no way she'd give him the power to do that again.

As for her attraction to him? She was a normal woman in her late twenties with needs, sexual needs, that had been long neglected. Noah was a gorgeous specimen and very capable of assuaging those needs. Her attraction to him was a simple combination of horniness and nostalgia and curiosity. It didn't mean anything; it couldn't mean anything.

He was a family friend, no more, no less.

A family friend with sexy arms, muscled shoulders and strong, strong legs. And a face that he could've inherited from a fallen angel.

Crap.

"Jules? Is your dating going to pose a problem to us working together? To acting like my other half around Paris?"

Jules blinked and shook her head, pulling her attention back to his question. "No, not at all. I'm not in a relationship with anyone."

"Okay, good. To keep things simple, I suggest that we never meet with Paris together, that one or the other deals with her, you on the interiors, me on the design."

Jules thought that he was onto something. There was no point in giving Paris any ammunition. And this way, Paris couldn't comment on their relationship. Or nonrelationship. Or, to put it another way, lie.

"That sounds like a plan," Jules agreed. "When does she want to meet with me?"

"As soon as possible, this week if we can arrange a time. Paris has a habit of forgetting meetings and darting off to Madrid or Mexico."

Yeah, she was familiar with the socialite's modus operandi. When Jules had designed her house, she'd have workmen waiting to start, waiting for Paris's final approval only to find that the blasted woman was at a spa in Monte Carlo.

One step at a time, Jules thought. "Let's start with what you imagine the interior of the yacht to look like."

"You don't want to get a brief from the client?" Noah asked, surprised.

"Normally I would, but Paris changes her mind on a minute-by-minute basis. Trust me, she's easier to handle if you don't give her the whole box of crayons to play with."

Jules walked over to her tote bag and bent over the side of the chair to pull a sketchbook from its depths and thought she heard a low groan from behind her. When she whipped her head around, she saw Noah staring at the floor, his clenched fist resting on his thigh. "You okay?" she asked, heading back toward his desk.

Noah's eyes flew up and Jules almost took a step back at the leashed power in his gaze. He rose, slowly and deliberately, and the air in the room disappeared. That power she saw on his face, in his eyes, was pure, undiluted desire. For her.

Holy hell.

The sketchbook slipped from her fingers as Noah's

hands gripped her hips, as his masculine, fresh scent hit her nostrils and her chest banged against his. She couldn't stop her body's instinctive move to push her breasts into his chest, her hips aligned with his and… Yeah. There it was. Long. And hard. All for her.

Using her last few remaining brain cells, Jules slapped her hand against his chest, trying but failing to push him away.

"If you're going to be my fake girlfriend, I want one real kiss."

"Not a good idea, Noah."

"Screw good ideas," Noah whispered, his mouth descending to hers. His words whispered over her lips, and his eyes bored into hers. "Every time I've seen you since I came back, I've wanted to kiss you. It's bizarre but I keep wanting to check whether I imagined the power in our kiss. I don't sail much anymore, Ju, and kissing you is the closest I've come for months to feeling that same adrenaline."

God, how was she supposed to resist? He was all man, so sexy, and in his arms she was the woman she'd always wanted to be. Strong, sexy, powerful, feminine. But they shouldn't be doing this, it so wasn't a good idea…

Noah's mouth on hers kicked that thought away and all Jules could think about, take in, was that Noah was kissing her. He kissed like a man in his prime should, a man who was fully confident with who he was and how to make a woman feel incredible. He took and devoured, and just when she thought she might dissolve into a heap of pure pleasure, he toned it down, went soft and sexy, tender. He built her up, eased off, built her up again.

Sexually frustrating but soul-tinglingly wonderful. This…*this* was what she'd been missing from every other man who'd held her, kissed her. None of them made her core throb, her heart liquefy. No man before him made her feel intensely feminine, indescribably powerful yet, simultaneously, willing to be sheltered and protected. He made her feel everything she should.

Everything that she shouldn't.

She should step away and if he'd been demanding or insistent Jules might've done that, but Noah's hands didn't move from her hips, he didn't push his erection into her, didn't bump or grind. He just used his tongue and lips and, yeah, his teeth to maximum effect. Man, he was good.

Jules had no reservations about touching him, freely allowing her hands to sneak up under his shirt, exploring the thick muscles of his back, the ridges of his stomach, his flat, masculine nipples, the trail of hair that led down, down. She avoided his shaft, knowing that if she touched him there, if he touched her breast or between her legs, they would be making love in front of a clear window looking out to a busy marina.

But, damn, she was tempted…

Noah groaned deep in his throat, his mouth eased off hers and then his forehead was against hers, his eyes closed. "Crap," he muttered.

Crap indeed. Jules knew what he was thinking, he

didn't need to voice the words. Like her, a part of him kept hoping that the attraction that had flared to life so long ago would dissipate at some point but... No.

It was still there. Hotter and brighter than before.

Noah's fingers dug into her hips. "Being your boyfriend and not being able to have the benefits of the title is going to be harder than I thought."

Because she was on the point of saying "To hell with it, let's get naked," Jules forced herself to step back and pushed her hand into her hair. "That shouldn't have happened. Nothing is going to happen, Noah."

Maybe if she kept saying it often enough the thought would sink into their stubborn heads.

Noah used one finger to push a curl off her cheek. "It just did, Ju. We can't deny that there's something bubbling here."

"I wasn't going to deny that. But we're not going there, Noah," Jules said, feeling that familiar wave of stubbornness sweep over her.

"Why not? We're adults. It doesn't have to mean anything."

Jules nailed him to the floor with a hard look. "Sex might not mean anything to you, Noah, but it does to me. It's not a way to scratch an itch, a way to pass some time." She shrugged. "I only share my body with men I can trust, Noah. And, unfortunately, you're not that man anymore."

Jules ignored the flash of emotion she saw in his eyes, determined to ignore her inner voice that insisted that she'd hurt him, and bent down to pick her sketchbook off the floor. Holding it against her chest, she rocked on her heels. "I think we need some time to wrap our heads around the events of this morning."

She needed some distance from him, from the passion still swirling between them. "I'm going to go, but if you can send me the yacht's blueprints, I can put something together and we can thrash out a proposal to present to Paris."

Noah rubbed the back of his head and nodded. "Sounds like a plan."

Jules was grateful he didn't argue. "And when we meet again, it will be as professionals, Noah. This can't happen again."

It was Noah's turn to look stubborn. And frustrated. Jules could relate. "I can't just act like I'm not attracted to you, Jules, nor can I forget that you were once my best friend. I can't treat you like just a colleague."

Jules pulled her bag over her shoulder as sadness wrapped its cold self around her heart. "When you chose to walk out on us, on our friendship, you made anything deeper impossible, Noah. You neither gave our attraction, nor our friendship, a chance. I tried to salvage what we had, you didn't even meet me halfway. It was your choice, Noah, and you have to live with the consequences."

Jules, feeling sick and sad and, dammit, totally sexually frustrated, walked to the door. "I'll call you when I have something to show you."

Jules forced her feet to walk out the door, down the hallway. She just managed to throw a cheerful "'bye" to Levi and wave to Meredith. It was only when she passed through the access control gate and pulled her sunglasses over her eyes that she allowed a few annoying tears to escape.

She thought she was done crying over Lockwood, dammit.

Darby pushed her shoulder into the doorjamb and Jules met her eyes in the long freestanding mirror. Her sister was dislodging strands of hair from her messy bun every time her head moved. Dressed in low-slung sweats and a tank top, Darby shouldn't have looked so damn gorgeous, but she did. Her fraternal twin could wear a burlap sack and make it look like haute couture.

"So, another date?" Darby asked, her wide smile in place but her eyes showing concern.

"Nothing serious. Robert has been bugging me to have dinner with him for a while so I called him up and told him I was free tonight." She'd dated Robert the year before Noah left. He'd always been far more invested in their relationship than she was and Jules had hurt him when she'd finally called it quits. He was a nice guy, a kind, gentle man who'd been her first real boyfriend and her first lover.

"I thought you said you weren't going to go to dinner with him, that you didn't want him to think that there was any chance of you hooking up again."

That was before Noah returned and placed her heart, mind and body on a Tilt-A-Whirl. Jules refused to meet Darby's eyes. Hell, she was having trouble meeting her own. The only reason she called Rob was because she wanted to feel back in control, on firm footing and, because she was hoping for a miracle, a little part of her prayed that she'd look at him and magically fall in love with him. She knew Rob, knew how to handle him, what to expect. With Rob she'd be in control. He was safe and predictable…

Everything that Noah Lockwood wasn't. God, she was so pathetic.

Embarrassed at her behavior and her lack of maturity, Jules didn't answer her twin. She had to pull herself together, dammit!

Darby walked into Jules's bedroom and sat down on the end of her king-size bed, covered in blindingly white linen. Darby pulled her legs up and wrapped her arms around her knees, her slate-gray eyes curious.

"Where did you disappear to today?"

"I just needed some alone time."

After leaving Noah's office, Jules had needed to walk and then to run. Because she always kept a fresh set of gym clothes in a bag in the trunk of her car, she'd decided to head out of town to the Blue Hills Reservation to work out her frustration on a long trail run. After doing eight miles, she'd spent the rest of the afternoon sitting on the bank of the pond.

She'd kissed Noah. And she'd more than liked it. Holding her pencil in her hand, her sketchbook on her lap, she'd stared at the scenery, not seeing much beyond the blue sky and the forest. She was more interested in the movie playing in her head…his masculine, fresh-

tasting mouth doing crazy things to hers, his strong
body pressed up against hers, his warm male skin under
her fingertips, the sounds of approval and desire he
made deep in his throat. She hadn't been able to stop
thinking about what they did, his hard body and what
it all meant.

And when she couldn't think about that anymore,
when those thoughts became too overwhelming, she allowed herself to wander back in time, to sitting on her
parents' roof with Noah, talking about anything and everything. The goofy text messages they exchanged, the
way their eyes would cut to each other as they shared a
joke no one else was privy to. She was extremely close
to Darby and to DJ but Noah understood her on a fundamental level they didn't.

What could these kisses, the intense attraction between them mean? Where was this going, what were
they trying to be? Jules looked at her twin, unable to
tell her sister—the person she shared everything with—
how close she'd come to begging Noah to do wild and
wicked things to her on the floor of his office. How she
was both horrified and thrilled by the let's-get-naked-
immediately thoughts that bombarded her whenever
Noah stepped into a room.

"Jules, talk to me."

She couldn't, not today. Her feelings for Noah, her
need and her resistance were too overwhelming to be
discussed. But, because she was obligated to inform
Darby of any developments in the business, and because

it was a good way to change the subject, she could tell her about Paris. "I took on a new client today."

Darby looked surprised. "You don't have time for a new client."

So true. "It's Noah. His new client wants me to design the interiors of her yacht, is insisting upon it. My involvement has become a deal breaker so I said yes."

"I didn't think Noah could be pushed around."

So only Levi knew about the turmoil between Ethan and his stepsons? Jules wanted to explain the situation to Darby but it wasn't her tale to tell. She'd always kept Noah's secrets—the few he shared with her—and always would. "This project is important to him."

Darby shrugged. "It's your call, Jules, but be careful of burning yourself out. You are working extremely long hours as it is."

Jules knew Darby was mentally measuring her stress levels, whether she'd lost or gained weight, whether she was as healthy as Darby wanted her to be. A college basketball player and a sports fanatic—she'd moved on from triathlons and was now into CrossFit—Darby was a health nut. Her twin no longer ate processed food and most carbs or drank coffee. She'd also stopped eating chocolate! Chocolate, for God's sake!

Jules didn't know how she got through the day.

"Blow Robert off, Jules, and come to The Tavern with us."

"That would be rude." And being in The Tavern would make her think of all the fun nights she'd spent there with Noah. Plus there was a good chance that Levi or his brothers would drag him to the bar tonight and she'd spend the evening trying not to beg him to take her to bed. The day had been long and hard enough as it was.

"May I point out that you only ever run away when you don't want to talk, and the only time you don't want to talk is when you are confused? And the only time I've seen you confused about a man is with Noah. So, did he kiss you or what?"

In the mirror, Jules watched herself turn a bright shade of tomato red. *Ah, crap.* How could she lie now?

Darby approached her from behind and wrapped her arms around her waist. Bending down, Darby rested her chin on Jules's shoulder. In the mirror, gray eyes met pure silver. Darby shook her head, a small smile touching her lips.

Darby was looking inside her and reading all her unspoken thoughts. "It's just an attraction, twin."

Darby squeezed her gently. "I'd believe that if there wasn't a whole lot of substance beneath the sexy. And you both have it in spades."

Five

Noah...

Being back in The Tavern was like revisiting his youth. Nothing about the upmarket bar had changed in the years Noah had been gone. The staff still wore white shirts, black pants and red aprons, there were still the same elegant black-and-white photographs of Italy from the '50s and '60s on the wall, and Dom, the head bartender, was still behind the bar, a little grayer, a little fatter, just as attentive. Noah recognized a few of the patrons and knew that, as Bethann's son, most recognized him. Grandpa Lockwood might've conceived the idea of the country club, but his mom had developed the estate's facilities and she built and designed the two restaurants, this bar, the gym and the handful of shops to serve the estate which now, cleverly, included a coffee shop serving light meals.

Being back at The Tavern with his brothers, Levi, DJ and Darby was so normal and, damn, it was good to feel normal again, to be wearing faded blue jeans instead of designer pants, flat-heeled boots and a T-shirt instead of an expensive button-down and loafers. The bar inside the club had a stricter dress code—business casual—but this was a place for the residents to relax, to blow off steam. In here he wasn't the professional sailor or the yacht designer; there was no one he needed to impress.

Everything he enjoyed most—the cold beers, good music, easy laughter and companionship of people he'd known all his life—was in this room.

Well, except for Jules.

Noah took a sip of his beer and looked across the room, idly watching Dom pour red wine into a glass. He wanted to go back in time, to when Dom was younger, to before he understood Ethan was more concerned about money than his stepsons. He wanted to rewind to when Jules looked at him like he was a superhero, when he was young and blissfully unaware of the crap storm coming his way.

While it felt wrong for Jules not to be there, a part of him was grateful. Since kissing her this morning he'd been unable to concentrate, to focus. He'd tried to distract himself by having lunch with Eli and Ben, and Ben's latest blonde. He'd exchanged eye rolls with Eli at her baby-girl voice and take-care-of-me-big-boy attitude. Because they were in company, they avoided talking business and it was a relief to delay telling his brothers he was working with Jules. There would've been questions: Are you friends again? What happened to cause the great rift? Did you behave like a dick? What did you do to piss her off?

He'd have to have a conversation with them about Jules at some point. He might only be in Boston for a short period but none of them—because the Lockwoods were one of Boston's founding families and because Callie and Ray had been most A-listy of A-list couples—were low profile. Before one of them heard the red-hot gossip that he and Jules were dating, he needed to give them a heads-up and, at the very least, some sort of explanation.

Hell, they wouldn't have to wait to hear the gossip, put him and Jules within ten feet of each other and sparks flew. And that would raise more questions and speculation...

The best way to douse those sparks would be to avoid her, but that was impossible. Apart from the so-called fact that they were "dating," they were also now working together; he'd sent Paris an email confirming Jules's commitment to the project. While he was in Boston the next month or two, and because his friends and family were hers, they were going to be living in each other's pockets. And trying to keep his hands and mouth off her was something he didn't seem to be able to master. Kissing her wasn't nearly enough... Limiting himself to a few kisses was like giving a drunk the smallest sip of whiskey, waving the glass in front of his nose while keeping his hands bound to his sides.

Having Jules, kissing Jules and not being able to take it to its natural conclusion was a cruel and unusual punishment.

Speaking of punishments…he'd never grasped how much he'd hurt Jules, how much his departure had affected her. He'd been so caught up in his own grief, misery and, yeah, homesickness that he couldn't think about those he left behind. Apart from the odd email and phone call back home, he focused all his attention on the present, on winning his races, being the best damn sailor he could be. Emotional distance, the ability to step away from a situation and focus, became a habit. Those traits, and the need to keep busy, kept him winning races, as many as possible as soon as possible.

Winning, disconnecting, moving forward was an entrenched habit, but here in Boston he was battling to connect with his cool, rational, thinking side. He had Jules to thank for that.

Levi jammed the end of a pool cue into his side. "Can you, at the very least, acknowledge that I'm kicking your ass?"

Noah looked at the pool table and cursed. Only a few balls remained, and if Levi sunk those, he'd be handing over some cash. He was out of practice.

Levi bent over the pool table, eyeing his shot. Noah was surprised when he lifted his eyes to lock with his. "Anything I need to know about? You seem distracted."

He could lie but this was Levi. He could justify not

telling his brothers—they were younger than him and this was none of their business—but Levi was Jules's brother. And a protective one at that. If he was going to open this can of worms, it had might as well be now.

"Just the past smacking me in the face." Noah lifted his beer bottle to his lips. "This life is very different from the one I've been leading."

"High-end clients and cocktails," Levi said after taking his shot, the five ball rolling into the far right pocket. Damn.

"Pretty much," Noah agreed. "This, a simple evening playing pool with my mates, is something I haven't done in years."

"Your fault, not ours," Levi said with his characteristic bluntness. "We were here."

He couldn't argue with that. Noah put his beer bottle onto the high table and rested his hands on the top of the cue. He needed to say this, had to get it out. "Lee, Jules and I—"

Levi held up a hand and his face turned dark. "Oh, hell, no! I don't want to know."

And he didn't want to spit the words out but he had to give Levi a heads-up, he owed him that much. But how to gently tell him that he wanted his sister with a ferocity that terrified him was turning out to be harder than he thought. He mentally tested a few phrases but none of them sounded right and all of them would end up with him sporting a broken nose. So he settled for simple. "Paris Barrow thinks we are dating—long story—but I should tell you that something is cooking between us."

Levi rolled his eyes. "That's the best you can do?"

"I'm trying to avoid a trip to the emergency room," Noah admitted. "So, yeah, that's all I can say."

Levi stared at him while he made sense of that statement. When he did, his expression darkened. "I need brain bleach." Levi bent over his cue again, stood up to speak and bent down again, frustration radiating off him in waves.

He stood up, tossed the cue on the table, dislodging the few remaining balls. "Crap, Noah! She's my sister and you are my oldest friend. I should punch you just for looking at her, but then you might piss off again and we might not see you for another decade!"

Underneath the frustration he heard anger and, worse, hurt. His absence hadn't only affected Jules, it had touched Levi, as well. And, he surmised, Eli and Ben and, to a lesser extent, DJ and Darby.

He didn't even want to know what Callie thought about his time away...

Levi's punch to his shoulder packed restrained power and rocked Noah back onto his heels. "Don't mess this up, Noah. You hurt her and we'll have words. We're partners and that will make for a tough atmosphere. Be very, very careful, because one wrong move will have consequences."

He knew that. God, he wasn't an idiot.

"Thanks for spoiling the game and my mood, dude," Levi said and stomped off toward the bar.

Crap. *Good job, Lockwood.* His phone vibrated and when he pulled it out of his pocket, he read the name on his screen. Morgan. Dammit.

Hi. Where are you? Would you like to get together for a drink for old times' sake?

It took Noah two seconds to type out a solid, in caps NO. After pressing Send, he shut his phone down and slipped it back into the pocket of his jeans. Not now. Not ever.

He'd rather chew his wrists off than allow her back into his life. The fact that she was spectacularly beautiful and amazingly good at sex had confused his twenty-three-year-old brain and he'd stayed with her far longer than he should have. Jules had detested her from the moment they met and the feeling had been mutual. Trying to juggle his best friend and girlfriend had been a pain in his ass. But as time went on, the sex became wilder and Morgan became clingier, and Jules more disparaging about their relationship.

Fresh air wafted toward him and Noah turned to look at the open door. All rational thought evaporated as he took in Jules's teeny-tiny dress and ice-pick heels that made her legs look longer than should be legal. Black material skimmed her curves and fell from a round neck over perfect breasts, leaving those creamy shoulders and toned arms bare.

Not knowing whether he could take much more, Noah lifted his eyes to her perfectly made-up face, her extraordinary eyes dominating the rest of her features. Her mouth, frequently ignored because her eyes were so startling, was covered in a light gloss and he wanted to pull that plump bottom lip between his teeth. She'd subdued her hair into some wispy, complicated roll, and diamond studs glinted in her earlobes.

Mine, his body shouted. *Mine! Mine! Mine!*

Calm the hell down, caveman, his brain replied. *You don't believe in love, or commitment.* And, as he'd learned from his mom and Ethan, love made people act foolishly and lose control. He had no intention of following in their footsteps. He was more than happy to learn from the mistakes of others.

So, instead of walking over to her, throwing her over his shoulder and kissing her until she screamed with pleasure, he turned at the sound of amused female laughter and looked into DJ's lovely face.

DJ grinned. "Watching you two has always been one of my favorite forms of entertainment."

Jules...

Jules stepped into the always busy bar and instinctively made her way to the back right-hand corner, where the gang always made themselves at home. Yep, they were all there. Darby was leaning across a pool table, about to make an impossible shot, Eli was looking resigned at losing some more money to her, and Levi and DJ had their backs to the wall, beer in their hands. Ben was wedged between two blondes at the bar and he didn't look like he wanted, or needed, rescuing.

Same old, same old...

Jules wove her way between the tables, greeted a few regulars and smiled at Dom behind the bar. Then she looked back to the billiards area and her heart belly flopped when she noticed Noah standing in the shadows, looking hot. He was the reason she'd rushed through her dinner with the still-pleasant Rob, the reason she'd kept checking her watch. Noah was the reason she steered her car here instead of heading home. She was a pigeon and he was her homing device.

Because that thought annoyed and irritated her, Jules indulged her inner toddler and ignored Noah, pretending not to notice the way his broad shoulders filled out that designer T-shirt, the way his jeans clung to his muscular thighs and outlined his impressive package perfectly. Before Noah, her eyes had never dropped below a guy's belt. Jules's cheeks heated and she closed her eyes, mortified.

Only Noah could make her feel so out-of-control crazy.

As if he could feel her eyes on him, Noah swiveled his head and their gazes collided, a million unspoken thoughts arcing between them. Jules, because she could read him so well, managed to decipher a few heading her way. *I want you. I missed you. God, you're hot. This is complicated.*

Did he still have the ability to read her eyes? Would he be able to discern that she was terrified of what him returning to Boston meant, scared that he would hurt her again? Would he see her wishes that they could go back, that he would kiss her again, that he would show her how spectacular sex could be?

The flash of awareness in Noah's eyes told her that he received her this-is-crazy-and-we-should-stop messages.

They really should. Jules watched Noah approach her and desperately wanted to thread her fingers into that thick hair, feel that blond stubble against her lips, feel him rock himself against her core.

What they should do and what they were going to do were two vastly different things.

Noah...

Noah handed Jules a G&T, heard her quiet thank-you and leaned his shoulder into the same wall Jules had her back against. She smelled fantastic, but beneath her smoky eyes and expertly applied makeup, she looked frazzled. And exhausted.

Like him, she was working long hours and if she was going home to lie awake fantasizing about how they would burn up the sheets, he could sympathize. When he finally fell asleep on those long nights, he often woke up with a hard-on from hell, his mind full of her, throbbing with need.

God, he was so tired of solo sex.

"Darby looks like she's cleaning up," Noah said, trying to distract himself from images of Jules naked, under and on top of him. "When did she get so good at pool?"

Jules smiled and he saw the kid she used to be, fun loving and so damn naughty. "Darby dated a pool player in college and she spent hours being coached by him. She said it was the only way she could get any of his attention. As a result, she got really good at it. And Deej and I are really grateful for her skill."

There was more to this story. "Okay. Why?"

"Throughout college Darby hustled guys who assumed she was just a pretty face and her winnings always funded our bar bill. Some of her bigger bets also paid for a few beach and skiing weekends away." Jules took a sip of her drink and smiled. "As you know, Mom and Dad put us on a budget. If we wanted money to party and play, we had to work for it."

For all their worth, and it had been considerable, Ray and Callie believed in making their kids work for their money. His mom learned that from them, too; he and his brothers were expected to work at the club as golf caddies or, while he was alive, for Grandpa Lockwood at the marina. At the time he'd resented putting in the effort, but those long summers spent busting his butt taught him the value of hard work. He couldn't have achieved his sailing and financial success without knowing how to put his head down and graft. Jules wouldn't have built a business without it either.

If he ever had kids, it would be a lesson he'd pass on.

Except having kids, getting married—or getting married and having kids—wasn't part of his plan. Designing Paris's yacht, buying back this estate and leaving Boston was. Jules wasn't part of the plan either. Noah looked at his watch and saw that it was nearly midnight. He hadn't planned on staying this late and had work he wanted to complete tonight, but when Jules arrived, he knew he wasn't going anywhere. Standing next to her, breathing in her scent, was where he most wanted to be.

And staying later meant more drinks and he was pretty sure that he was close to the limit. Damn, he wouldn't be driving himself home tonight and that meant either asking one of his brothers for a lift. Except that Eli had left Darby to talk to a redhead in the corner and Ben was... Well, Ben was gone—so that meant he would be catching a cab.

Noah pulled his phone out of his back pocket and powered it up. After he plugged in his code, his phone lit up like a Roman candle on the Fourth of July.

"You're a popular guy," Jules said, and he heard the snark in her voice. The possibility of her being jealous gave him an unexpected thrill.

Noah stifled a smile and scrolled through his messages. One from Paris, a few from his team back in London and four, five, seven from Morgan. "Crap on a cracker," Noah muttered, scowling.

"Problem?" Jules asked, lifting her finely arched eyebrow.

Having nothing to hide, he held up his phone so that she could see his screen and the various missed calls and notifications from his ex.

"Wow," Jules said, eyes widening.

"Yeah, did I tell you that the reason I named you as my girlfriend was because Morgan has put it out there that she wants us to get back together?"

Jules dropped her head and ran her finger around the rim of her glass. "Is that a possibility?" she asked quietly.

"I'd rather get smacked repeatedly in the teeth by a flying boom," Noah stated flatly.

There was that small smile, the one he'd been looking for. Jules lifted her head and he saw the relief in her eyes, and a hint of humor at his quick response. "So why does she think that's a possibility?"

"Because she's deluded?"

Jules smacked him on the arm. She thought he was being sarcastic or, worse, rude about Morgan's issues. He rubbed the back of his neck. "I wasn't joking. She actually is bipolar and she also has some other mental health problems. Her dad described her to me as being 'emotionally fragile.'"

He'd been thinking about calling it off when Morgan had had her first proper meltdown, staying in bed for two weeks, not eating or drinking or, God, bathing. She'd bounced back from that episode and he'd decided to give her some time to recover before he broke up with her.

But every time he distanced himself, she went into a decline and he genuinely worried for her. When she was healthy, she was a fun partner and, well, yeah, the *sex*. Her skill between the sheets was partly to blame—

along with too much whiskey—for him agreeing to even entertain the idea of commitment.

Her father had worked fast, offering him exactly what he needed when he most needed it. Two years passed and when he was released from his sponsorship deal with Wind and Solar, the first thing he did was visit Morgan and formally end their engagement. Why he bothered, he didn't know since they were both leading very separate lives. But he did the deed and a week later Ivan sent him a brief text message stating that Morgan was in the hospital and that they both blamed him for her nervous breakdown.

He'd tried to let her down gently. He'd seen Morgan a handful of times over those two years they were supposed to be engaged and, within a month of him leaving Boston, their twice-a-week phone calls fizzled to once a month and then to one every couple of months.

He sent her the same emails he sent everyone else and Ivan paid for her to visit him in various ports as he raced, but those visits became, thank God, rarer and rarer. The cash kept coming in from Wind and Solar and he kept the few liaisons he had time for very low-key and trouble-free.

Amazing that, ten years later, when he was supposed to be so much wiser and mature, he was in another fake relationship, but this time with Jules. Maybe life was finally realizing a fake relationship was all he was capable of.

Jules, as he expected her to, looked shocked. "Wow. That's... Wow." It took a moment but then her natural curiosity and frankness reasserted itself. "I still don't understand why you became engaged to her. I know you didn't love her—" Jules's eyes dropped from his and he saw her swallow "—like that."

He'd never loved a woman, not like that. And he never wanted to. What could be worse than thinking someone loved you, lived and would die for you, only to find out that you'd been played for a fool and what you thought was love was something else? The concept of love was too nebulous, too open to interpretation.

Jules looked like she was waiting for an answer and Noah wasn't sure how to respond. Reticence was a habit he couldn't break, not even with Jules. Besides, his fake engagement to Morgan wasn't exactly something he was proud of but it had been the best choice at the time. "There were reasons, Jules. Can we leave it at that?"

Jules's chest rose and fell, and when she finally lifted her face to look at him, he saw profound sadness in her eyes. She opened her mouth to speak but then shook her head and remained silent. He shouldn't ask but the words left his mouth despite his best intentions. "What were you about to say, Ju?"

Jules scraped the last of the gloss off her bottom lip with her teeth. Then she bobbed one shoulder. "I was just thinking that we used to tell each other everything but then I realized that wasn't true. I used to tell you everything but you didn't reciprocate. You were very selective with what you wanted me to know and, as an adult, I can recognize that now. But it still makes me sad."

God, didn't she realize that he told her more than

most, that she, at one time, knew him better than anyone else? "I did talk to you, Jules. As much as I could," he quickly added as a qualifier. "Besides, talking about boyfriends and how mean or unreasonable our parents were wasn't exactly life-and-death stuff."

"It was more than that and you know it," Jules protested.

Yeah, it had been but he couldn't think about that now. Because remembering made him want to go back to when his life was uncomplicated, to that time when his mom was alive, his father loved him and life was golden. His biggest worries were what amateur race to enter next, getting his assignments in on time, dating that cute blonde in his marine systems class.

"Whatever it was, we can't go back, Jules. We have to deal with the here and now," Noah said. God, he was tired and, yeah, sad. This was the downside to being back in Boston, hanging out with his family and people who knew him well. He couldn't insulate himself from emotion, distance himself when conversation turned personal.

It wasn't easy to do when he was talking to someone who'd lived across the road for most of his life. He'd desired other women, of course he had—he was in his thirties and had always enjoyed a healthy sex life—but there had never been anyone whom he thought about constantly, whom he, let's call it what it was, *obsessed* over. Even in his teens he'd never spent this amount of emotional energy thinking about a girl.

He was so completely and utterly screwed. And because he was on the point of saying to hell with it and throwing caution to the wind—and his obsession at her feet—he thought that it might be a good idea if he took his ass back to his boat.

Yep, Eli was on his way out with that redhead, so his only options were a taxi or to sleep on the couch at Jules's house. Not that he would sleep knowing that Jules was upstairs, in that comfortable bed...

An expensive cab ride it was, then.

Super.

Six

Jules...

Jules sat in Noah's visitor's chair and propped her bare feet up on his cluttered desk. Leaving her sketch pad on her knees, she dropped her thick pencil on top of the pristine paper and lifted her arms to gather her hair and twist it into a knot. She picked up a lime-green pencil from the small table next to her elbow and jammed it into her hair, working the pencil in to keep it all up.

She darted a look at Noah sitting at his high desk, black-framed glasses resting on the bridge of his nose. His brow furrowed in concentration as his hand flew between his notepad and a desktop calculator. Every now and again, he scribbled something on the plans spread out in front of him.

Hot damn, sailor. Or a hot sailor, damn. Both worked in Noah's case.

Seeing that Noah was concentrating on his blueprints, Jules pushed her hands under the large sketch pad and pulled her tight skirt up her thighs so that she didn't feel like she was sitting in a fabric tube. An improvement, she thought. Jeans or jammies would be miles better but she'd left the Brogan and Winston offices earlier that day to meet Noah and Paris at Joelle, a see-and-be-seen cocktail bar that was housed in one of the chicest boutique hotels in Back Bay. Possibly in the city. They'd thought that it would be better for Jules to meet Paris on her own but their client had declared them a unit and insisted on a "Team Paris" meeting. Her words, not theirs.

While Paris downed margarita after margarita, she and Noah tried to nail down Paris's wishes, expectations and desires for her yacht and its interior.

Two hours and four margaritas later, none of which had, sadly, passed their lips, they still had nothing. They were, however, handed a glossy invitation to a soiree Paris was planning at the end of the month. "Just a few friends, darling. Casual chic, be there by seven."

Through experience Jules knew *casual chic* could mean anything from ball gowns to beachwear, and seven actually meant later—much, much later. Everybody knew to add an hour or two onto Paris's stated time.

Jules tapped the point of her pencil against the white paper, leaving tiny dots on the surface. "She wants it to feel open but also cozy. Sophisticated but relaxed. But mostly, it has to look like it cost a fortune."

Noah lifted his head to look at her. Or rather, he looked at her after he eyed quite a bit of her exposed thigh. Jules thought about tugging her skirt down but then Noah would know that she noticed him checking out her legs, and he might also realize that she liked him looking at her legs. *Aargh!*

Noah straightened and lifted his arms in the air to stretch, pulling his button-down shirt across his ridged stomach and wide chest. Through the white cotton she could, if she stared hard enough, see his flat brown nipples. Jules couldn't stop her eyes from skating over his stomach, over his pleasing, and promising, package to look at his thighs covered by his gray suit pants. They'd be tanned and, as they'd been since he was fourteen, corded with muscle. Pleasantly furry.

Man, her old friend/new colleague was seriously *hawt*. As in smokin'.

And...none of this was helping her with her other problem, her real problem of not knowing what the hell Paris wanted.

Jules dropped her head back and groaned. "I need inspiration."

Noah stood and rested his hands on his hips. "How can I help?"

Jules lifted her head up and rubbed the back of her neck. "Did Paris say anything to you about the interiors when you first spoke to her about designing the yacht? Was there anything in those conversations that could steer me in the right direction?"

Noah thought for a minute. "Not really. She told me to design something that would make her friends drool. Gave me the budgeted figure and said to come back to her when I had some thoughts. I've managed to pin her down to some specifics—what she wants the boat for, cruising the Caribbean and possibly the Med, and for entertaining, which means big reception and deck areas. Her eyes glazed over when I mentioned anything to do with engineering or design." Noah frowned. "'Design a boat, here's a small deposit to get you started, make it spectacular.'

"I don't think she's very interested in sailing."

Jules laughed at his deadpan comment. "What makes you think that?" she quipped. "So, tell me about the boat."

Noah walked around the desk to her and perched his butt on the corner of his desk. "I sent you the blueprints. All the specs are in there."

"Yeah, but I have no idea what the boat actually looks like. Maybe I can take some inspiration from your design…"

"I didn't send you the concept drawings of the yacht?" Noah asked, sounding shocked by his inefficiency.

"Nope."

Noah frowned again before walking back to his drafting table and pulling a folder out from underneath his blueprints. Flipping it open, he removed a sheaf of papers and returned to his spot on the desk. Stretching out his long legs, he handed Jules the sheaf of papers, a hint of nervousness in his eyes. It almost seemed like Noah was seeking her approval, that he wanted her to like his work.

Strange, since Noah was the most self-assured man she knew.

Jules looked down and her breath hitched. Despite the roughness of the sketch she could see the fluid, almost-feminine lines of the yacht, the gentle curves, the sensuous bow. Moving on to the paper below, Jules tipped her head to the side. Noah took his rough design to his computer and the color printout in her hand looked like a real, already built yacht, just ten times more beautiful than the concept drawing.

Sleek, elegant, feminine…spectacularly well designed.

"Oh, my goodness, Noah, it's…" Jules couldn't think of an adjective that adequately contained how wonderful she thought his design was. She sighed, slumped back in her chair and looked into Noah's intensely masculine face. "It's… Wow."

"You like it?"

"Are you kidding me? It's gobsmackingly, shockingly beautiful. I have no words."

Pride flashed in Noah's eyes. "I like it."

"You should." Jules tapped her nail on the glossy paper. "You've put so much thought into the design, you know exactly what you want the interior to look like."

Noah nodded, so Jules picked up her sketch pad,

found a clean page and picked up a bright pink pencil, prepared to make a list.

"I thought about echoing the fluidity of its lines with a feminine interior," Noah said, "but by *feminine*, I mean sleek and sexy as opposed to frilly and fancy."

Yeah, she understood. Long lines, gentle curves, no harsh edges.

"I'd like comfortable white furniture with pops of color. Bold pinks or oranges or reds, feminine colors but strong tones. There are a lot of windows to show off incredible views so we have to consider the sea an accessory."

Noah tossed more suggestions at her and Jules wrote quickly, struggling to keep up with him. Interesting textures, hidden flat screens, storage space. He'd thought about it all. He eventually ran out of ideas—thank goodness because her hand was starting to cramp—and gripped the edge of his desk with both hands, his intense eyes locking with hers. "Make it feminine, sexy but soft. Accessible but with a hint of mystery. Look inside."

Her head jerked up at his last sentence and the air between them turned thick and warm. "What do you mean by that?" she asked, unable to disguise the rasp in her voice.

Noah's intensity ratcheted up a notch and… *Zzzz*… She was sure that was the sound of her underwear melting. "I look at the yacht and I see you. Sexy, slim, so damn feminine."

"Noah." Jules pulled his name out into three, maybe

four, syllables. It was a plea but she wasn't sure what she was asking for. *Please kiss me* or *please don't*? *Please stoke the fires and make me burn* or *please hose me down*?

"What do you want, Jules?"

Nothing. Something. *Everything*.

Jules was unable to answer him, and when a minute or two passed—or ten seconds, who knew because time was irrelevant—Noah surged to his feet. Tossing her sketch pad to the floor, he gripped her biceps, lifted her up, and up again, so that her mouth was aligned with his. Still holding her, his mouth touched hers…sweet and hot and sexy and… *Dear Lord.*

Jules wasn't sure how his arms came to be around her waist and how her skirt got high enough to allow her legs to wind around his hips. All she knew was that her core was pressed against his impossibly hard erection, her nipples were pushed into his chest and his mouth was turning her brain to slush.

She didn't want to be anywhere else.

For years she'd been kissing guys who made her feel something between mild revulsion and "mmm, this is okay" but nobody turned her into a nuclear reactor like Noah did. Nobody had ever made her feel she'd choose making love to him over dodging a missile strike or a tunnel collapse. If she got to touch and be touched by Noah, she'd take her chances.

Oh, man, she was in so much trouble.

Noah's hand ran up the back of her thigh, over the bare skin of her butt. "A thong. Nice."

It would be so much nicer if he got rid of that tiny scrap of material that called itself underwear. "Take it off." Jules spoke the words against his lips, dipping her hands into the space between his pants and his lower back, wanting to go lower, to feel his butt cheek under the palm of her hand.

Noah pulled back, his eyes intensely focused. On her, on making her his. She wanted that, to belong to him again, if only for this moment in time. "Jules…"

She knew what he was about to say and she didn't want to hear it. Yes, it was a bad idea. Yes, they'd only just reconnected. Yes, there was a lifetime behind them and they had no idea how to navigate the future. But she wanted this, wanted to know Noah before they re-established their friendship. Because the yacht project had them spending so much time together, she couldn't keep him at arm's length, even if she wanted to. Which she didn't. She wanted Noah back in her life, the hole in her heart was finally closing. They were on their way back to being friends.

God, she hoped he knew there couldn't be more between them, that this night and a burgeoning friendship was all they could have. They'd make love, get it out of their systems and accept that they could never go beyond a casual friendship.

Because, as nice as it was to have Noah back in her life, she was never going to open up to him again in the way that she did when she was a child, then a teen. She'd trusted him once and he'd abused that trust when he left her, stayed away without so much as an explanation for an entire decade.

Noah was going to leave again; it was what he did, and this time she wasn't allowing her heart to leave with him.

But sex, pleasure—yeah, she trusted him with her body. If she wanted to know passion, and she did, then it had to be now, today. Tomorrow could take care of itself.

"I want this, Noah. I want you."

He opened his mouth to argue but Jules didn't give him a chance, she just molded her lips against his and slipped her tongue inside his mouth to slide against his. She heard his deep, feral growl, felt his fingertips push into the skin of her butt. When the thin cord of her thong snapped, she knew she'd won the small argument.

Or that Noah had let her win. She didn't care.

"One time," Noah muttered, pulling away from her mouth to push his lips against her neck. "One time and we get over this."

Jules nodded her agreement and briefly wondered if Noah knew she would agree to selling her kidney on the black market if it meant making love to him. She was under his spell...

Or for the first time ever she was finally experiencing the joy of really, really good foreplay. And if foreplay was this intense, sex itself was going to be fan-damn-tastic.

Suddenly she couldn't wait. She put a little distance between their bodies and attacked his shirt buttons, needing to see him, feel him. Whoops, button gone. Oh, well, tit for tat since her tattered thong was lying at their feet. Her thong was forgotten as Noah's hand ran up the inside of her leg, skating past her core, making her squirm.

Jules spread his shirt apart and placed an open-mouthed kiss against the skin above his heart. Noah. God, she was making love to Noah. Suddenly scared, she rested her forehead against his chest, her hands on his belt buckle but making no attempt to divest him of his pants.

Was this a mistake? She was sure it was...

Noah's hand stilled. "Second thoughts?"

"Yes? No... I don't know."

"If you want to stop, we can pretend this never happened. Or we can carry on and pretend this never happened. Either way, in the morning this can all be a wonderful dream or a fantastic memory."

"Do you want to stop?"

Noah's strangled chuckle rumbled across her hair. "Honey, I have a sexy woman in my arms, the one I've fantasized about since I first tasted her luscious mouth a decade ago. That kiss changed everything and I've been wanting to kiss you, taste you there and everywhere, since then. Hell, no, I don't want to stop."

Jules looked up at him. "You thought about me?"

Noah used one finger to push her hair off her forehead and out of her eyes. "More than I should've. I imagined you naked and responsive and the reality is a million times better than the dream."

"How can one kiss change us?"

"God knows," Noah said, lifting his hand to pull her silk T-shirt out of the band of her skirt. His hand trailed over her rib cage before covering her breast, his thumb pulling the lace of her bra over her already aching nipple.

"Stop or carry on, Jules? Tell me now."

She wanted this. It was just one time and they'd forget it happened in the morning. Or was she deluding herself? When dawn broke, forgetting anything wouldn't be easy to do but she was willing to find any excuse, clutch any straw to be with Noah. To know him intimately.

Thinking that actions would say more than words, Jules gripped the edges of her T-shirt and slowly pulled the fabric up her torso, revealing her lacy white bra. She heard Noah's intake of air, and when she looked at him, his eyes were on her breasts. Using one finger, he gently rubbed one nipple before transferring his attention to the next.

"I guess that's a yes."

"A huge fat gaudy yes," Jules responded huskily.

Jules gasped when Noah grabbed her hand and pulled her across the room and into a space between the wall and his drafting table. Pushing her into the corner, he placed her back to the wall and undid the front clasp of her bra. Then both her breasts were in his hands and she groaned. "As much as I like that, want to explain why we are in this corner?"

"Windows. Marina. Can't see us here," Noah muttered, bending to suck her nipple. A hot stream of lust hit her core and Jules moaned. Noah couldn't use long sentences and she couldn't speak at all.

Lord, they were in a world of trouble.

To hell with it. Nothing was hurting now. And she wanted more. She wanted it all.

Jules reached for Noah's pants, undid his belt buckle and managed, somehow, through luck rather than skill, to flip open the button to his pants. Jules was very conscious of his erection under her hand and she couldn't resist running her fingers over his length, imagining him pushing into her body, slowly and, oh, so deliciously. She slid the zipper down and then pushed his pants over his hips, wrapping her hand around his shaft and skating her thumb across its tip.

Noah cried a curse and lifted her skirt to bunch it around her waist. They were half-undressed but they didn't care, nothing was more important than having him fill her, stretch her, make her scream.

"Condom," Noah muttered.

Protection. Yeah, that was important. Noah reached behind him and patted the desk, grunting when his hands closed around his wallet. Pulling it to him, he flipped it open, digging beneath the folds. Eventually, he pulled out a battered foil packet that Jules eyed warily.

"That looks old."

Noah ripped open the packet and allowed the foil to float to the floor. "It'll do the job."

That was all she cared about. Jules tried to help him

roll the latex down his length but Noah batted her hands away. Covered, his hand slid between her legs and Jules shuddered. *Oh, God, yes. There. Just like that.*

"Do you like that, sweetheart?"

"So good." Jules spiraled on a band of pure, undiluted pleasure and lifted her head, looking for Noah's mouth. He kissed her, hard and demanding. Noah lifted her thigh over his hips and plunged inside her. Feeling both protected and ravished, Jules had the sensation of coming apart and being put back together as Noah worked his way inside her, as if she were spun sugar and liable to break.

"Noah," Jules murmured, her face in his neck, trying to hold on. In another dimension, Jules heard the vibrant ring of his phone. Focused on what Noah was doing to her, making her feel—she'd never believed it could be this magical, this intense—Jules ignored the demands of the outside world, but when the phone rang again she tensed.

Noah clasped her face in one hand, using his thumb to lift her jaw so that their eyes clashed and held. "You and me, Jules. The rest of the world can go to hell."

Jules nodded as he pushed a little deeper, a little further and she whimpered. She wanted more, she needed every bit of him. "So good, No. You feel amazing."

"It's going to get better, Ju. Hold on."

"Can't. Need to let go... Oh, God."

Noah stopped moving. Jules whimpered and ground down on him, wanting to set the pace. Jules thought she heard Noah's small chuckle but then he was moving, sliding in and out of her, the bottom of his penis rubbing her clit and she was done. The world was ending and it was...

Stars and candy and electricity and fun and...

Mind-blowing. And emotional. Tears pricked her eyes and she ducked her head so that Noah didn't see the emotion she knew was on her face. This was only supposed to be about good sex, great sex, but here she was, trying to ignore that insistent voice deep inside claiming this was more, that it always had been, that she was a fool if she thought they could be bed buddies and brush this off.

This is Noah, that voice said, *your best friend, your hottest fantasy. He's not just some random guy who gave you the best orgasm of your life. He's the beat of your heart—*

No! No, he wasn't.

Those feel-good hormones were working overtime, her serotonin levels were making her far too mushy. She could not allow herself to allow the lines between sex and love to blur, to mix it up with friendship and good memories to make one confusing stew. Sex was sex; friendship and love had nothing to do with this.

She wouldn't allow thoughts of love and forever to mess with her mind. She was smarter than that.

Noah...

Sex against the wall with his onetime best friend. He was not proud. Noah ran a hand over his face, listening as water hit the basin in the bathroom adjacent to his office. He hadn't intended that to happen...

Liar, liar...

He hadn't been able to think of much else than touching Jules—tasting her, sliding into her warm, wonderful heat—since he'd returned to Boston. And since he was being honest, he could admit, reluctantly, that he'd told her the truth when he'd said that he'd often thought about doing that and more since their decade-old kiss. He'd sailed many oceans and had spent many long nights, waves rolling under the hull, imagining doing just that.

But not up against a wall. Not for their first time... That was all types of wrong.

Noah tucked his shirt back into his suit pants and ran his hands through his hair. He dropped to his haunches and picked up Jules's sketch pad, smiling a little at her girlie, swirly handwriting. He closed the book, picked up the colored pencils that had rolled off the table and placed them on his desk. What now? Where did they go from here?

Noah looked at the closed door and wondered what was going through Jules's smart head. Hell, what was going through his? Not much since he was still trying to reboot his system. All he was really sure of was that sex with Jules was the best he'd ever had and, yeah, he'd had his fair share. He'd been single all of his adult life and sex wasn't that difficult to find.

But that had been a physical release, some fun, something he enjoyed while he was in the moment but rarely thought about again. Jules, sex with Jules, was not something he was going to be able to dismiss as easily. Or at all.

Yeah, it happened at the speed of light—something else he wasn't proud of—but he had a thousand images burned into his brain. Her eyes turned to blue the wetter she became, her brows pulled together as she teetered on the edge. The scar on the top of her hand, the perfect row of beauty spots behind her ear. Her mouth, the combination of spice and heat, feisty just like she was. Her scent—he'd never be able to smell an orange again without becoming mast hard. She'd ruined citrus for him...or made it ten times sexier.

And, God, how was he supposed to work twelve inches from where he'd had the best orgasm of his life? Unless he moved his desk, his concentration would be forever shot. In the morning he'd move his desk to the opposite corner. There wasn't as much light and the view was crappy but he'd manage to get some work done.

Or maybe he was kidding himself. Just having Jules back in his life was a distraction he didn't need.

He needed her to complete this project… She was red-hot at the moment and was in the position to pick and choose her clients. Paris wanted her and only her.

Once Jules produced her portfolio of design ideas for Paris to look at—hopefully she'd fall in love with one of the proposals, and quickly!—Paris would sign off on the design and a hefty pile of cash would hit his bank account. He'd use that money for the down payment on the house. He already had a preapproved mortgage in place to tide him over until he sold his apartment in Wimbledon and George paid him out for his share in their yacht rental business in Italy.

Ridiculous that he had many millions in assets but, thanks to the timing of other investments, he was experiencing a temporary cash flow problem.

Up until fifteen minutes ago he was also experiencing a sex flow problem.

His phone vibrated on his desk, and Noah picked up the device, wishing the damn things had never been invented. He saw the missed call from earlier, frowned at the unfamiliar Boston number and saw that his caller had left a message. Dialing into his voice mail service, he lifted the phone to his ear, keeping one eye on the bathroom door.

"I cannot believe that you would embarrass me this way! Paris Barrow told me that you are seeing Jules Brogan! How dare you, Noah? Her of all people! Why didn't you just take out a banner ad stating that I meant nothing to you?"

Noah looked at the screen, cut the call and shook his head. Getting harassed by your ex was a very good way to chase away any lingering fuzzies. It was also a great way to kill the mood.

Crap. Ignoring Morgan, leaving her long text messages unread and not confronting her directly was not getting his point across. It didn't matter whether he was in a fake relationship with Jules or neck-deep in love with her or anyone else, what he did and who he did it with was nobody's business but his own. He was going to have to meet with his ex and explain to her, in language a five-year-old could understand, that his love life was firmly and forever off-limits.

Noah rubbed the back of his neck. Obviously his return to Boston had flipped Morgan's switch.

The door to the bathroom opened and Noah saw the resigned but determined look on Jules's face. Nothing had changed.

Having sex up against the wall—hell, having sex—was going to be a onetime thing.

Damn. Crap. Hell.

Jules rubbed her hands on her thighs before folding her arms, causing her breasts to rise. And, yep, his IQ just dropped sixty points back to caveman mentality. "So, that happened," Jules said, darting a glance at the corner. Judging by her trepidation, he expected to see that the wall had caught alight.

And how was he supposed to respond to that? Yeah, it happened. He wanted it to happen again... Next time in a bed.

"Not one of our smartest moves, Lockwood."

And here came regrets, the we-can't-do-this-agains. Jules lifted her tote bag off the floor and brushed past him to pick up her sketch pad and pencils. As he pulled in a breath, he smelled that alluring combination of sex and citrus, soap and shampoo. All girlie, feminine Jules in one delightful sniff. His junk stirred.

"I'm going to head home. It's been a long day."

It had but, thank baby Jesus, it ended with a bang.

Noah gave himself a mental kick to the temple for the thought. It was asinine, even for him. He frowned, wondering when she was going to spit out what she was actually thinking…

This isn't a good idea. This can't happen again. Let's pretend I didn't get nailed against a wall and that it wasn't the most head-exploding, soul-touching sex of my life.

Jules half smiled as she held the sketch pad against her chest. "Let me work with what you gave me and hopefully I'll have a couple of sketches, sample materials for you in a couple of days. Will that work for you?"

What was she rambling on about?

He'd left stubble burns on her neck, her blouse was incorrectly buttoned up. Noah wanted to undress her, take her on the desk and then, when he was done, he'd dress her again. Properly this time.

Or maybe he'd just hide her clothes and keep her naked.

"Noah?"

Jules looked at him as if expecting an answer. What the hell did she say?

"Oh, God, you're getting weird. I didn't want us to act weird," Jules muttered, shifting from foot to foot. "Are you waiting for the other shoe to drop, the sky to fall down? Relax, I'm not going to ask what this means, whether we can do it again. I'm fully aware of your bam-wham policy."

Bam-wham… *What?*

"What are you talking about?" Noah was impressed that he managed to construct a sentence that had the words in the right order.

Jules patted his chest, much like his mom had to placate him when he was ten. "It's all good. No. That was something that had been building to a head for ten years and it needed to erupt. Now we can go back to doing what we do best."

"And that is?" And why did he sound like he had a dozen frogs in his throat?

Jules's smile was just a shade off sunny. "Being friends." Jules patted his arm this time and it took Noah everything he had to not react. "I'm out of here. I'll talk to you in a day or two, okay?"

Noah watched her walk out of his office and two minutes later, heard her run down the metal stairs to the ground floor of the building. Hayden, the marina's night manager, would make sure she got to her car safely so he could stay here and try and work out what the sodding hell just happened.

And, no, it most definitely was not okay.

Jules...

Ladies and gentlemen, the award for Best Actress goes to Jules Brogan.

Oh, why couldn't sex with Noah have been meh and blah? Why did it have to be skin-on-fire, want-more wonderful? It had taken a herculean effort for Jules to turn her back on Noah and leave the office. Now at the bottom of the stairs leading to the reception area of the marina's office, she ignored the burning urge to retrace her steps.

She and Noah didn't have a future. They never had. He was only in town long enough to complete this project and within a few weeks, maybe a month or two, he'd be gone again. If she didn't keep her distance she would be staying behind, holding her bleeding heart in her hands. This time she wouldn't only be mourning the loss of her friend but also her lover.

She'd cried enough tears over Noah, thank you very much.

As more tears threatened to spill, Jules could only pray that Noah wouldn't follow her in order to continue their going-nowhere conversation. And situation.

She couldn't allow history to repeat itself; that was just stupid. They needed to keep their relationship perfunctory and professional. Two words that weren't associated with sex.

What had she been thinking... Had she been thinking at all? Their kiss so long ago had knocked them out of the friends-only zone and had, admittedly, rocked her world. How could she possibly have thought she could handle sleeping with him?

Then again, when Noah touched her, when his eyes darkened to that shade a fraction off black, her brain exited the room and left her libido in charge. Her libido that hadn't seen much action and couldn't be trusted to make grown-up decisions.

Jules waved off the night manager, who offered to walk her to her car, and stepped into the warm night. Pulling in a deep breath, she waited for the night air to clear her head. Walking down the marina, reason and sanity returned.

Use that brain, Brogan.

She wasn't living in Victorian times; this wasn't a catastrophe. She was fully entitled to have sex with and enjoy a man, his skills and his equipment. This didn't have to mean anything more than it was: a moment in time where they did what healthy adults did. It was sex, nothing more or nothing less.

A fun time was had by all up against the wall.

She wasn't a poet, nor was she a liar... Jules sighed. Despite her brave words to Noah and her insouciant attitude, sex did mean something to her, sharing her body was a curiously intimate act. She never slept with men unless the relationship was going somewhere...and, because there hadn't been many contenders to feature in her happily-ever-after life, she was a shade off being celibate.

Sleeping with Noah had been an aberration, an anomaly, a strange occurrence.

Jules pushed through the access gate to the marina, turned to look back at the double-story office building and blew out a long, frustrated breath.

She couldn't sleep with him again. It was out of the question. He'd hurt her, disappointed her, and she couldn't trust him not to do that again. Erecting a wall between them was the smart, sensible course of action. It was what she had to do.

So why, then, did it take her five minutes to open her car door and another ten to start the car and drive home?

Seven

Callie...

Callie hugged DJ and Darby, and then pulled Jules into her arms, keeping her there for an extra beat, wishing she could ask Jules to stay behind, to demand that Jules tell her why she'd spent most of breakfast staring out of the window of the coffee shop, her thoughts a million miles away.

"Are you okay, baby girl?" Callie whispered in her ear.

Like she did when she was a little girl, Jules rested her forehead on Callie's collarbone. "I'm fine, Mom."

No, she wasn't, but this wasn't the time to push and pry. Not when there were so many ears flapping,

Darby's, DJ's and also, dammit, Mason's. She'd intro-
duced him to her daughters and he'd been courteous
but professional, thank God. Points to him that he kept
his flirting between them.

Enough of him, this was her time with her daughters
and she wasn't going to waste a minute of it thinking
about Mason. Callie's eyes flicked across the restaurant, saw that Mason was looking at her, and she shook
her head. Distracting man! He wasn't, in any way that
counted, her type. Too young, too good-looking, too…
poor?

God, she was such a snob! She had enough money
to last several lifetimes and it wasn't like Mason was
penniless. He had a good business, looked financially
liquid. She'd never judged men, or anyone, by their bank
balance. Why was she doing it with him?

Because she was looking for any excuse, poor as it
was, to keep her distance.

It didn't matter, nothing was ever going to happen
between them! Irritated with herself, Callie stepped
back and framed Jules's face with her hands, sighing
at the confusion she saw in her eyes.

There was only one thing she could say, just one
phrase that she knew Jules needed to hear. "Just keep
standing, honey. Keep your balance until it all makes
sense."

It had been Ray's favorite piece of advice, one he'd
used his whole life. And, except for him dying when he
was supposed to be retiring, it mostly held true.

"I needed to hear that, Mom." Jules managed a small

smile. Then the smile evaporated and pain filled her eyes. "I miss him, Mom."

"I do, too, honey," Callie said, touching Jules's cheek with her fingers.

Callie walked her to the door, holding her hand. At the door she hugged her girls again and caught Mason's gaze over Jules's shoulder. His blue eyes were on her, a curious mixture of tenderness and heat. Damn that lick of heat spreading through her!

Jules stepped back and when she smiled, mischief danced in her eyes. "He's really good-looking, Mom."

That point had crossed her mind a time or two. Callie opened the door and ushered her brood outside. Shaking her head, she retraced her steps to her table, sat down and pulled her notebook out of her bag. Flipping it open to the first page, her eyes ran down her bucket list.

She'd moved to a new house in a different section of the estate so she could tick the first item off her list. She squinted at number two. Seeing tigers in the wild meant planning a trip. Was that still what she wanted to do?

"Learn a new skill? Bungee jump? Have phone sex?"

Callie heard the voice in her ear and when she whipped her head around, she found Mason's face a breath away, his sexy mouth hovering near hers. Callie wanted to scream at him for reading her private list but her tongue wouldn't cooperate. Then she felt his thumb stroking her back, while his other hand was on the table, caging her between his arm and his chest.

So close, close enough to kiss.

"Do you know how much I want to taste you right now?" Mason murmured.

"Y-you read… It was private," Callie stuttered, mortified. Her cheeks were definitely on fire. She'd mentioned sex! On her list! Now Mason knew she wanted some… Callie looked around the coffee shop, convinced that a million eyes—people she played bridge and tennis with—were all watching them, somehow knowing that she wanted to kiss Mason more than she wanted to breathe.

God, she was losing her mind.

"I'll tell you what's on my bucket list if it makes you feel any better," Mason replied, his hand moving up her back to cup her neck, the heat of his hand burning into her skin.

"You're probably just going to steal my ideas and call them yours," Callie muttered.

Mason's eyes flicked down to the list and Callie slammed her hand down on the page to cover her writing.

"I've traveled, thrown myself off a bridge on a rope, don't need another job. Wouldn't mind another trip somewhere." He smiled and Callie's stomach flipped over. "I have had one-night stands, wouldn't recommend it."

Callie placed her face in her hands and groaned. "What are you, some sort of mutant speed-reader?"

Mason's laugh raised goose bumps on her skin. "Only a few items are on my list, Callie."

Callie scowled at him. "Do I even want to know?" She placed a hand on his shoulder to push him away but got distracted by the muscles bunching underneath his polo shirt. *Nice...*

Seeing that she was stroking him like he was expensive velvet, she yanked her hand away and, yes, dammit, blushed again. "Back up!"

Mason flashed her a smile and jerked her pen from her hand before picking up her notebook. Flipping to a new page, he pulled off the cap of her pen with his teeth and started writing.

He flipped the page back to her list, wrote some more and handed the book back to her. Callie looked down, noticing that he'd placed asterisks next to her "have a one-night stand" and "have phone sex" bullet points, drawing a line from both to what had to be his phone number.

Her face turned so hot she was sure that her skin was about to reach meltdown temperature. Mason skated his fingertips down her cheek before sending her a slow smile and turning away.

After a few minutes of resisting the urge to peek— she was embarrassed enough as it was—Callie turned the page and saw Mason's so-called bucket list. It was comprised of just three bullet points and a sentence.

Take Callie on a date.
Make her laugh.
Kiss her good-night.
See previous page for additional suggestions.

Clever, sexy man. A very dangerous combination.

Jules...

Since arriving at Whip, an exclusive cocktail bar situated in a boutique hotel on Charles Street, Noah had looked on edge. His jaw was tight and his eyes were a flat deep brown, suggesting that he was beyond pissed. But why? What had happened? What had she done?

"Are you okay?" she asked, jabbing her elbow into his side.

"Fine," Noah said through gritted teeth.

Jules sighed. Since their conversation the other night at The Tavern, Jules now saw their past a little clearer and remembered having to badger Noah to open up, to tell her anything. He was one of those rare individuals who internalized everything, preferring to rely on himself and his own judgment to solve his problems.

Unlike the rest of the clan, Noah had refused to openly discuss girls, college, his problems. The best way to get Noah to talk had been to join him on the back roof of Lockwood House and refuse to budge until he'd opened up. That was how she found out that his tenth grade girlfriend had dumped him, that he was going to study yacht design, how he was dealing with news that his mom had been diagnosed with pancreatic cancer.

But if she'd struggled to make him speak up on a thirty-foot-high roof back when they were friends, there was no chance of him opening up to her in a crowded room heaving with people who considered eavesdropping an art form.

Jules accepted Noah's offer to get her a drink from

the bar and, standing by a high table, looked around Whip. She took in the deep orange walls, the black chandeliers, the harlequin floors. The decor was up-market and vibrant... She approved. Just like Darby studied and commented on buildings, critiquing decor was an occupational habit for Jules.

Jules looked at Noah's broad back, saw that he would be waiting at the bar for a while and, feeling anxious, tapped her tiny black clutch bag on the table. By mutual, unspoken agreement, they'd given each other some space this past week, hoping to put some distance between them and their hot, up-against-his-office-wall encounter. She hadn't thought about him a lot, only when she woke up, ten million times during the day and when she went to sleep at night.

Jules sighed. Despite her busy days and her insane workload, the urge to touch base with Noah was at times overwhelming. A random thought would pop into her head and the only person she wanted to share it with was Noah. She'd be out and about, see an innovative light fixture or an interesting face and she'd reached for her phone, wanting to tell Noah about what she'd heard, done or seen.

A part of her thought she was sliding back into the habits of her younger self, to when she'd been in constant contact with Noah, but this was something more, something deeper. Every time she forced herself to cut the call, to erase the already typed message, she felt like she was stabbing a piece of her soul, like she was fighting against the laws of nature.

Not being connected to Noah was wrong. But her instinct for self-preservation was stronger than her romantic self, so she kept her distance.

But, God, her heart leaped when she opened the door to him tonight. It threatened to jump out of her chest when he placed a hand on her lower back to escort her to the classic luxury car he'd kept locked up in the underground garage at Eli's apartment. She'd gripped the door handle to keep from leaning sideways and touching her lips to his, from threading her fingers into his hair.

Jules tossed another glance at Noah's back. She really needed that drink and the soothing effects of alcohol, though a swift kick in the rear might be equally effective.

Noah was off-limits. Today, tomorrow, always. She rather liked having her heart caged by her ribs and not walking around in someone else's hand.

"Jules Brogan?"

Jules turned and smiled when a still-fit-looking older man with shrewd green eyes and silver hair held out his hand to her. Jules tipped her head, not recognizing his face.

"Ivan Blake."

Okay, the name sounded familiar but she couldn't place him. The connection would, she hoped, come to her in a minute or two. "I hear that you are Paris's interior designer."

"For her yacht, yes."

"And I understand that you and Noah are seeing each other?"

Now, what did that have to do with him? Since she wasn't prepared to answer him, she just kept quiet and looked around the room. "You don't know who I am, do you?"

"Should I?" Jules asked him, her voice three degrees cooler than frosty.

"I'm Morgan's father."

And a million pennies dropped. "Ah." What else could she say? *I never liked your daughter, and I think she played Noah like a violin?* "Is Morgan here?"

Because her presence would really make this evening extra interesting. And by *interesting* she meant freaking awful.

"She wasn't feeling well so she decided to stay home."

Thank God and all his angels, archangels and cherubs.

"She's been trying to reconnect with Noah and she feels like you are standing in her way," Ivan said.

Jules nodded to Noah, who was standing a head and sometimes shoulders above many men at the bar. "He's a big guy, Mr. Blake, I couldn't stand in his way."

"You're missing my point, Miss Brogan."

Jules allowed her irritation to creep into her voice. "You're missing mine. Noah is a successful, smart, determined man. If he wanted to reconnect with Morgan, I wouldn't be able to stop him. And tell me, Mr. Blake, when is Morgan going to stop having her daddy fight her battles?"

"Morgan is fragile."

Jules wanted to tell him that Morgan was also manipulative, but she kept silent. Wanting to walk away but hemmed in by the crowd, she had to stand there and keep her expression civil.

"Would you be interested in doing some work for me?"

Jules's eyes snapped up at the change of subject. Say what? "Are you kidding me? Morgan would disembowel you if you hired me."

"Not if you distanced yourself from Noah to give her a chance to win him back," Ivan said, his voice both low and as hard as nails.

"I don't need the work, Mr. Blake."

"But your sister does. She's been looking for a breakthrough project for a while, a way to put her name out there, to allow her to work on bigger and more exciting projects. She needs a chance and you could give that to her.

"I'm on the board of a very well funded foundation dedicated to promoting the art and artists of this city. The foundation has acquired a building not far from the Institute of Contemporary Art which we intend to demolish and replace with another smaller art gallery and museum. We're looking for an architect to design the space," Ivan continued.

Dear Lord, that was so up Darby's street.

"Walk away from him, just like he walked away from you, and I'll put in a good word."

Wow.

Jules frowned at him, feeling like she was part of a

badly written soap opera. "You're kidding, right? People don't do this in the real world."

"Oh, they do it far more often than you think," Ivan said, a ruthless smile accompanying his words. "Just think about my offer. I'm prepared to give Darby a fair chance, maybe throw some design work your way."

"If I break up with Noah," Jules clarified, trying to stifle the bubble of laughter crawling up her throat. This was both too funny and too bizarre for words. He was offering Darby a huge project, a project that would catapult her career to the next level if Jules broke up with her fake boyfriend.

Again… Wow.

A part of her wanted to say yes; this man was offering her sister an opportunity of a lifetime. An art gallery and museum… Was he kidding? Darby would sell her soul to work on a project like that! Jules hesitated, conscious that she had yet to say no, that she *should* say no.

"Turning me down would be a bad business decision, Ms. Brogan. I can promote you and your sister, but the pendulum swings both ways."

And that meant what? He'd blackball and bad-mouth them? Jules tipped her head to the side and was surprised at the resignation she saw in his eyes. He didn't want to do this, act this way. The man was tired, emotionally drained.

"Why are you letting her push you like this?" Jules asked softly.

Ivan pulled in a deep breath, and sorrow and anger and fear mingled in his eyes. Ivan stared at her and was silent for so long that Jules didn't think he was going to answer or acknowledge her question. "Because," Ivan said, speaking so softly that Jules had to strain to hear his voice, "I'm scared that if I don't she's going to go a step too far."

Ivan ran his hand over his jaw and stepped back. "Let me know your decision, Ms. Brogan."

Before she could reply, tell him that she wasn't interested, Ivan Blake faded into the crowd, leaving Jules alone and wondering if she'd imagined the bizarre conversation.

"Have you seen Morgan?" Noah asked through clenched teeth.

Jules turned at Noah's voice and, not for the first, and probably not the last, time that night, noticed how good he looked in his black suit, slate-green-and-black-checked shirt and perfectly knotted black tie. Jules followed his eyes and saw that he was looking at Ivan Blake, his expression as dark as thunder.

He handed her an icy margarita and Jules took a sip. "She's not here, No. You can relax." His expression immediately lightened and his shoulders dropped from around his ears.

So his bad mood was due to his fear of running into Morgan. Now that made sense and it was something she could fully relate to.

"Thank God. And how do you know?" Noah replied, his hand wrapped around a tumbler of whiskey.

"Her father told me," Jules said.

"He spoke to you? What did he want?" Noah released a bitter laugh. "Oh, wait, let me guess. He wants you to break up with me."

No flies on her big guy. "Yep. How did you guess?"

"Because his daughter has been bombarding me with text and voice mail messages, begging to meet, to give her another chance."

Jules reached out, grabbed the lapel of his jacket and twisted the fabric in her fist. "You do that and I swear, I will drown you in the bay."

A small smile touched Noah's mouth and he removed his jacket from her fingers and smoothed down the fabric. "I'm not stupid. I got stuck in that web once. I'm not moronic enough to do that again."

"If she's hassling you, you need to tell her that, Noah."

Noah scowled. "I've been trying! I've asked her to meet. I even popped by their house but apparently no one was home. But I did catch movement behind the drapes of what was always Morgan's room."

"You know where her room was?"

Noah shrugged. "Sex." Ew. Jules shuddered but Noah didn't notice. "She's been trying to get my attention for three weeks and now she won't talk to me, answer the door?"

"Of course she won't. She knows you're going to tell her something she doesn't want to hear. Instead, she sent her father to try and manipulate the situation."

He wore his normal inscrutable expression but Jules

saw the worry in his eyes. "Would he be able to manipulate you?"

The urge to thump him was strong. "I'm going to pretend that you didn't ask me that."

"Sorry, but Ivan Blake has the ability to discern what people want or need and then push the right buttons to obtain his—or in this case, Morgan's—goal."

There was a story there and she'd ask him to explain, but first she wanted to go back a few steps, to get him to clarify an earlier point. Actually, thinking about it, it was still related to the topic at hand. "What did you mean when said you got caught in his web? As I said the other night, *you* stayed engaged to the girl long enough that she couldn't have been all bad."

"The sex was fantastic," Noah said, and Jules narrowed her eyes. He lifted up his hands in apology. "I was young and she was talented. But she was hard work."

"Again...you were together for nearly two and a half years! Why?" Jules demanded, knowing there was something she didn't understand, a huge puzzle piece she was missing.

Noah took a sip from his glass, his eyes never wavering from hers. "I never proposed to Morgan." What? Well, that was unexpected. Still, it didn't explain the long engagement.

Noah ran a hand through his hair and Jules noticed his agitation. Good, he should be agitated since he'd allowed whatever he had with Morgan—the supposedly fantastic sex, ugh—to get so out of hand.

"That Christmas Eve we had a discussion about

commitment, but I was drunk and exhausted and don't remember much of it. I woke up the next morning, sporting a hangover from hell, to this wave of good wishes on our engagement," Noah said, pitching his voice at a level only she could hear. "Getting married was the last thing on my mind.

"Then, now and anytime since," Noah added, his words coated with conviction.

His statement was an emotional slap followed by a knife strike up and under her ribs, twisting as it headed for her heart. She shouldn't be feeling this, there was nothing between them but a long-ago friendship, a few kisses and hot sex. Still, something died inside of her and in that moment, standing in a crowd of the best-dressed and wealthiest Bostonians, she felt indescribably sad and utterly forlorn.

She'd never imagined that Noah would live his life alone. Like his mom, he had an enormous capacity for love, provided he thought you were worth the effort. Once, a long time ago, she had been worth the effort. But that boy, the one who'd trusted her in his own non-communicative way, had loved her, of that she was sure.

This adult version of Noah, tough, stoic, determined, didn't. And he would never allow himself to. The thought popped into her head that if he wasn't going to marry, then neither was she, but Jules dismissed it as quickly as it formed. His decision had no impact on her future plans...

She hoped.

Annoyed with herself, Jules opened her mouth to

bring them back to the ever so delightful topic of his engagement to Morgan. "So why stay engaged, No? Fess up."

Noah rubbed his hand over his jaw, and Jules wondered if he'd tell her the truth or fob her off. "So, there I was on Christmas morning, nursing a hangover from hell, and before I could make sense of what I was hearing, Ivan handed me a massive sponsorship deal. It was three times bigger than any offers I'd received before, included a new yacht, an experienced crew."

Jules struggled to make sense of his words. "But you were sponsored by Wind and Solar."

"Which he has a controlling but little-known interest in," Noah explained. "He made me an offer I couldn't refuse."

"To drop out of college, to run away?"

Noah's jaw tensed. "That's your perception, not mine."

"You left me with barely a word and definitely without an explanation. You abandoned me and our friendship. You also broke your promise to your mom to look after your brothers and to finish college," Jules hissed.

The color drained from Noah's face and Jules wished she could take her words back. It wasn't like Noah left his brothers alone and defenseless when he went away ten years ago; Eli was already in college and Ben was about to start his freshman year. They both had a solid support system in her mom and dad and Levi, and could turn to any of them if they needed help or guidance.

His brothers had been fine but he did leave them. As

for finishing his education, his lack of a degree hadn't hurt his career at all, so who was she to judge? But it was just another promise he'd made that he'd broken...

We'll always be friends, Ju. There will never be a time that we don't talk. I'll always be there for you, Ju. You can rely on me...

She could and she had...until she couldn't. And didn't.

Noah drained his glass of whiskey. "Just to clarify... I finished my education. I didn't break that promise. I did my best to look after Eli and Ben. That was part of the reason I had to leave, why I had no choice but to take the—" Noah jerked his head in Ivan's direction "—asshat's offer. I'm sorry I wasn't around, Jules, sorry that I missed your dad's funeral, that I couldn't hold your hand. But, Jesus, I was doing what I needed to do!"

"You're not telling me everything, Noah."

Noah stepped closer to her, trapping Jules between the wall and his hot, masculine frame. Her traitorous body immediately responded to his nearness, and her nipples puckered and all the moisture in her mouth and throat dried up. He was using their attraction as a distraction from their conversation but Jules didn't care. Her need to be kissed was the only thought occupying her shrunken brain.

She shouldn't kiss him, because kissing was one small step from sleeping with him again, thereby narrowing that emotional distance she needed to keep between them. Jules placed her hand on his chest to push him away but her actions had all the effect of a ladybug's.

"We're supposed to be lovers, Jules. Can you damn well act like it?" Noah muttered, dropping his head so that his mouth was a hairbreadth from hers. Jules sighed, forcing her body to relax.

"You drive me crazy, Noah."

"Ditto, babe."

Noah's mouth skated across hers in a leisurely slide, his lips testing hers. Jules wound her arms around his neck, her fingers playing with the surprisingly soft hair at the back of his head, wishing that she could run her hand down his back, over his butt.

Noah tore his mouth off hers and pulled back, lifting his hand to her face. Holding her cheek in his hand, the pad of his thumb glided across her bottom lips and she shuddered, the sensation almost too much to bear. "Yeah, I far prefer soft and sexy Jules to spitting and snarling Jules."

Jules opened her mouth to blast him but Noah spoke before she could, resting his forehead on hers. "Wind and Solar offered me a hell of a deal but it came with a huge price… I was caught between a rock and a hard place."

Oh, she wasn't going to like what she was about to hear.

"After Mom's death, I needed a lot of money very quickly. Blake offered me more than I needed, but the catch was that I had to stay engaged to Morgan for two years, enough time to get her mentally healthy."

Well, hell. Jules was trying to make sense of his words, this new information, when she saw their client, a champagne glass in one hand and delight in her eyes, approaching them. "I'm here! Let the party begin. Come, come, there are people I want you to meet! Oh, Julia, you look delightful! Come, come…"

Eight

Noah...

Jules—why did people assume her full name was Julia?—looked sensational, and that was a huge, irritating problem since Noah had this uncontrollable desire to pull her from the room, find a private space and rip that very delightful, extremely frivolous dress from her amazing body.

He didn't know if her blush-pink-and-black lace dress was designer or not—he so didn't care—but it suited her perfectly, being both quirky and sophisticated. She'd pulled her hair up into a sleek ponytail high on the back of her head and her makeup was flawless, with her face looking like she wasn't wearing any at all.

His childhood friend, gangly and gawky, was gone and the sexy woman she'd morphed into made all his blood run south. Grown-up Jules was sunshine and hurricane, calm seas and storm surges, the beauty of a tropical sunset and the tumult of the Arctic Ocean.

Like the many seas he'd sailed, she was both captivating and fascinating, with the power to both soothe his soul and rip it in two. Excitement pumped through his body and he felt alive. Rediscovering Jules was like setting off across the Atlantic Ocean, not sure what type of sea or weather conditions he'd encounter but damn excited to find out.

Noah allowed himself the delight of watching Jules, long legged and sexy, as she followed in Paris's wake. He hadn't seen her since she left his office ten days ago and it was nine days, twenty-three hours and thirty minutes too long. He'd spent most of that time with half his mind on his work and the rest dreaming, lost in memories of how she felt, tasted, smelled.

There was action in his pants and Noah thought it would be a very good idea if he stopped imagining her naked so he didn't embarrass himself. He knew of a quick way to deflate his junk, so he scanned the room, looking for Blake. He needed to speak to Morgan's father, make it very clear to him, so that he could explain it to his daughter, that he'd rather swim in shark-infested waters than hook up with Morgan again. He was sorry that she was a little rocky, slightly unstable, but she was no longer his problem.

Jules smiled and his heart flip-flopped. Damn Paris and her ill-timed interruption.

What was going through Jules's head? Did she hear and understand that he'd needed the money, that he hadn't had another option? That he did what he needed to do because he was between the devil and the Bermuda Triangle? But if she did think that he was a money-grabbing moron, then it was no one's fault but his own.

He wasn't good at opening up, exposing his underbelly. Communicating wasn't his strong point; he preferred action to words. Even his brothers didn't know the extent of Ethan's treachery. They didn't know about his many affairs, the incredible amounts of money he spent on girls just hitting their twenties.

He'd kept that from them, thinking that they didn't need to be burdened with that knowledge. In hindsight, he should've gone to Callie and Ray, asked for their help, their advice.

But looking back, he hadn't asked for help, shared what was going on because if he had, they would've seen how hurt he was, how out of control and messed up he'd felt. And if he'd fallen apart back then, he didn't think he would have recovered. And maybe that was another reason why he'd been prepared to accept Ivan's offer, since it had given him the option to run away, to put some distance between him and his mom's death, Ethan's betrayal, the need kissing Jules had evoked.

When he was sailing, he had to be fully present—his crew's safety was his responsibility—and he had to compartmentalize. Standing back from the situation, from the emotions, had allowed him to function and had become an ingrained habit.

He was finding that difficult to do with Jules now. She was constantly on his mind and not always in a sexual way. He found himself wondering about the weirdest things—did she still make her own granola, refuse to eat olives, make those face masks with oatmeal and honey?—and fought the impulse to connect with her during the day, just to hear her voice, see her smile.

And he wanted her back in his arms, naked and glorious, more than he needed his heart to pump blood through his body.

Noah rubbed the space between the collar of his shirt and his hair and caught Jules's concerned frown, the "Are you okay?" flashing in her eyes. She was worried about him, and her thoughtful expression suggested that she was still mulling over their conversation. There was no way Jules would leave that subject alone; she wouldn't be satisfied with the little he'd told her. She'd have questions...lots of questions.

He was still debating whether to answer them or not. He wanted to, for the first time in, well, forever, he wanted someone else's perspective, another opinion. No, hell...

He wanted Jules's perspective, her opinion. Wanted it but didn't want to want it...

This was why globe hopping, dropping in and out of people's lives was so much easier. Noah did up his jacket button, pushed his shoulders back and centered himself. Introspection could wait for later, right now he needed to socialize, to earn his crust of bread. And that meant discussing boats and sailing, recounting the highlights of his career and listening to amateur sailors as they tried to sound like they knew what they were doing.

Noah had played the game long enough. He understood the value of networking; it was extremely likely that a number of Paris's friends might have a spare fifty million for a new boat and he wanted them to think of him to design their vessel. Yeah, okay, designing an expensive yacht had been more fun than he'd expected. Building and designing boats, all types of boats, was his passion and rubbing elbows with potential clients was crucial for his business.

So get your head in the game, Lockwood.

Noah squared his shoulders, looked around the room to find Jules and saw her staring at the back of a silver-haired man, her eyes wide with distress. Noah instinctively made his way across the room, determined to reach her. Keeping his eyes on her, he was nearly at her side when a low voice calling his name halted him in his tracks.

No wonder Jules looked distraught. He didn't even need to look at the man's face, he knew exactly who'd caused his heart to stop, his blood to freeze. What the hell was his stepfather doing back in Boston? Just before leaving Cape Town, he'd checked to see where Ethan was and had been told that he was in Cannes. That he intended to remain there for the foreseeable future.

His stepfather, because he was a contrary ass, was exactly where Noah didn't want him to be: in Boston, breathing the same air he was.

Noah's fists clenched and he searched for and then connected with Jules's sympathetic gaze. She didn't know how or why he was at odds with Ethan but her loyalty was first and foremost to him. Her support was a hit of smooth, warm brandy after a freezing day on the water.

"Keep cool," Jules mouthed, holding out her hand. Noah gripped her fingers and nodded, grounding himself before turning around to face his stepfather.

"Ethan."

It seemed to Noah that the whole room was holding its breath, waiting to see how this encounter played out. Then he remembered that no one outside of his brothers knew of his war with Ethan. Noah was used to keeping his own counsel and Ethan wouldn't tell anyone that his stepson had instituted legal proceedings against him. The world only saw what Ethan allowed them to see, and that was the veneer of a charming, rich man-about-town.

His hid his snake oil salesman persona well.

"Hello, son."

Noah gritted his teeth. He'd once loved Ethan calling him son, loved the fact that blood and genes didn't matter to him so the *son* felt like a hit of acid. Funny how having his and his brothers' inheritance stolen tended to sour the adoration.

It took everything Noah had to shake Ethan's hand,

to pull his mouth into something that vaguely resembled a smile.

"I thought you were in the South of France."

Ethan whipped a glass off a passing tray and smiled, his blue eyes the color of frost on a winter's morning. "I've been back for a month or so." Ethan sipped at his drink, not breaking eye contact with Noah. "As you know, I've put Lockwood Estate on the market."

Noah tightened his grip on Jules's hand. It was the only thing keeping him from planting his fist into his stepdad's face. "And as you know, I'm enforcing the clause that you have to offer it to us first, less twenty percent of the market value."

"My lawyer informed me. I find it tiresome having to wait." Ethan smiled the smile he stole from a shark. "If you don't manage to buy it within the prescribed time period, I'll still sell it to you."

"What's the catch?" Because there would be one, there always was.

"The marina. Give me the marina and twenty million and you can have the estate and all your mother's crap."

His mother's crap being the Lockwood furniture, the paintings, the silver. God, he wondered if there was anything left. Her jewelry, her collection of Meissen figurines?

He was going to kill him, he really was. While the house had sentimental value, the marina was a valuable asset and one that could easily be sold. And that was why Ethan wanted it. Yes, the estate was bigger and more valuable, but it would be harder to unload.

Ethan was doing what he did best, making life easier for himself. Jerk.

Ethan was exploiting Noah's love for Lockwood land and his family's legacy. It was a deal he could never, would never, agree to. Partly because he was done being exploited by his stepfather but also because Levi was now a full partner in the marina and wouldn't allow such a half-ass arrangement.

"Out of the question," Noah replied.

"Pity. I'd rather go broke than let you have the estate."

"Please, you're far too materialistic and vain for that," Noah replied, his harsh growl coming from deep within his throat. Red mist was forming in front of his eyes, and he was moments from losing it.

Punching Ethan would so be worth the assault charge…

"I have a plan B and if my life turns out the way I'm planning it to, I might take the estate off the market anyway. No matter what happens, I refuse to put another cent toward your mother's house. I'd rather watch it fall apart, board by board."

It was an empty threat, one that was verbalized purely to needle him since Noah knew the maintenance of the Lockwood house was paid for out of the profits from the country club and its facilities. There was no way the management company would allow the magnificent home to fall apart on the grounds of such an exclusive estate.

Noah tensed but Jules squeezing his hand kept his inscrutable expression in place. But, damn, it was hard.

Pulling her hand from his, Jules stepped between him and Ethan and smiled. Noah's protective instinct wanted her behind him but the quick shake of her head kept him from moving. She smiled but her eyes were deep-freeze cold. When she spoke, her voice held an edge he'd never heard before. Tough, compelling, hardass. "Uncle Ethan, it's been a long time."

Ethan's smile turned oily; the old man loved the attention of a pretty woman. The younger the better. That love of attention emptied his bank accounts faster than water ran from a tap. "I know that I should remember you, but forgive me, pretty lady—" *Pretty lady? Gag.* "—I don't... Wait! Jules Brogan?"

Jules nodded. "Hello."

Ethan flushed and ran a finger around the collar of his shirt. "I'm sorry about your dad."

"Not sorry enough to come to his funeral, though."

Ethan pouted. "Noah wasn't there either."

Typical Ethan, always trying to flip the tables and shift blame. "Noah was, if I recall, crossing the Indian Ocean at the time. What was your excuse for not being there for my mom, to support her when she lost the man who was your neighbor and friend for more than twenty years? The same woman who cooked for you and your boys for months before and after Bethann died, who took in your boys when they were on school breaks, who was more their parent than you were?"

"Uh…"

Noah wanted to smile at Ethan's red face, at the hunted look in his eyes. He saw Jules open her mouth to blast him again but seeing Paris approaching them, he gripped the back of her neck. Jules looked up at him and he shook his head, gently inclining his head in Paris's direction. Their hostess and client held a PhD in gossip and he didn't want them to star in her melodramatic account of their run-in with Ethan.

Noah's eyebrows flew up when Paris wound her arms around Ethan's neck before dropping a kiss on his temple. She grinned. "Surprise! My sweetie told me he hadn't spoken to you for a while, that you'd had a tiny falling-out so I thought this would be a perfect occasion for you two to kiss and make up!" Paris's eyes sparkled with excitement. "Ethan told me that he taught you to sail, Noah, and he's kindly offered to guide me through the process of designing and buying a yacht."

Noah's heart plummeted to the floor and nausea climbed up in his throat. Noah looked at Ethan and saw the malice in his eyes, revenge-filled amusement touching his mouth.

"Darling!" Paris said, dropping a kiss on Ethan's lips. "There is music so we must dance."

Ethan raised his glass to Noah and invisible fingers encircled Noah's neck and started to squeeze. "We'll speak soon…son."

Noah hauled in shallow breaths as they walked away, dimly hearing Jules's calling his name.

When he finally pulled his eyes to her face, he clocked her distress and concern. "Noah, are you okay?"

Noah shook his head. "Nope. Basically, what I am is screwed."

Jules...

Jules was still reeling from the unexpected encounter with Ethan—and she could only imagine how Noah felt. They'd left the soiree as soon as they could and the drive back to Lockwood was silent. Without a word, Noah opened her car door, escorted her to her front door and, in the dim shadows on the porch, stared down at her with enigmatic eyes.

She had a million questions for him, a need to dig and delve, to understand the past, but it was late and clarity wasn't what she most wanted from Noah right now. No, this wasn't about what she wanted but what she needed to give him...

A couple of times at Whip she'd looked his way and while he seemed to be talking, having a good time, she'd sensed that it was all one damn good performance. He played the game well but she could tell that Noah was played out, mentally and emotionally. For the first time she appreciated how hard it was for him to return to Boston and to face his past.

Jules glanced across the road to Lockwood House, looking hard and menacing under the cloudy sky. He'd come home to buy his inheritance back but dealing with his past had to be harder than he imagined. She'd assumed that his spat with Ethan had been just that, a spat, an old bull, young bull thing, something that would blow over. She hadn't really noticed that Eli and Ben didn't speak about their stepfather much; he was always out of the country, and because he was a sailor and yachtsman, she'd assumed that Noah had more contact with Ethan than they did.

That was a mistake. Noah loathed Ethan, and Ethan returned his antipathy.

Something fundamentally destructive had occurred to cause such unhappiness...

Noah placed a hand on the door above her head and looked down at her, his face as hard as the house over the road. "It's been a long and crappy evening, Ju, I don't want to talk about it or answer any questions."

"Fair enough," Jules replied, placing her hands flat against the wooden front door behind her. Arching her chest, she looked up at him, deliberately lowering her eyes. She knew what Noah wanted and it was the one thing she could give him, what she wanted—no, needed—as much as he did. To step out of their complicated lives and feel.

Warm skin, wet lips, heat...

Noah's voice was low but rough. "I want you. But you know that already."

"I do." Jules nodded, hooking her hand around the back of his neck. "And I want you, too. Take me to bed, No. Take me away to a place where our passion is the only truth."

"Nothing changes, Jules. As soon as I buy Lockwood, I'm still leaving," Noah stated quietly, still looming over her.

His blunt statement hurt, of course it did, but it didn't distract her from wanting what they both craved. "Kiss me, Noah."

Judging by his hard eyes and tense body, Jules expected to be hurtled to mindlessness by hard and fast sex. So his soft kiss, the tenderness in his touch, surprised her.

Noah bent his knees, placed an arm beneath her bottom and lifted her so that her mouth was aligned with his. Her feet dangled off the floor, but it didn't matter because Noah was holding her, exploring her mouth, seemingly desperate to taste her. Her breasts pushed into his chest and she shifted her knee, brushing against his erection.

Yum...

Noah allowed Jules to slide to the floor, silently demanding the key to the door. She licked her lips and shook her head, her brain stuttering. Noah released a frustrated sigh, reached for her clutch bag and flipped it open. His fingers delved inside and he withdrew the key, handing the bag back to her and stabbing the lock all in one fluid movement.

Impressive, since she wasn't sure how to spell her name. "How can you think, act? All I can think about is how wonderful you make me feel."

Noah gripped her wrist and jerked her inside. "I'm motivated. I've been imagining ripping that dress off you all evening."

Okay, that statement pierced the fog. But…no. As much as she wanted to get naked, this dress was too expensive to be a casualty. She slapped her hand on Noah's chest. "Do not harm this dress, Lockwood."

When he just smiled at her, Jules slapped him again to make her point. "Seriously, Noah. Don't do anything to this dress."

Noah held up his hands before his expression turned, and she saw determination, tenderness and a great deal of fascination in his face. He touched her cheek and his fingers trailed over her jaw. "You are so damn beautiful, Jules."

Jules touched her tongue to her top lip. When he spoke in that reverent voice, his confidence and cockiness gone, she saw Noah at a deeper level, stripped bare. She liked the softness beneath the bad-boy layer, the tenderness beneath his alpha facade.

She liked him. She loved him. And in ways she shouldn't.

Determined not to go there, not to think about that now, Jules closed the front door and linking her fingers with Noah's, led him up the stairs. She smiled as they both instinctively avoided the steps that creaked, staying to the side of the hallway to muffle their footsteps. They were adults but they were acting like her parents still occupied the master suite down the hall.

Jules led Noah into her bedroom, shut the door and kicked off her heels. Turning around, she looked at her man, taking a moment to watch him watch her. Deciding that her dress needed to go—because she didn't fully trust that wild look in Noah's eye—she reached under her arm and found the tab to the hidden zip, slowly pulling it down her side. The dress fell apart and Jules, enjoying this striptease more than she thought she would, slowly stepped out of it, draping it over the back of her chair. In the corner of her eye she caught her reflection in her freestanding mirror, saw her strapless, blush-colored bra and matching high-cut panties. Her underwear covered as much as her bathing suit normally did but she looked wanton, like a woman anticipating her lover.

And, dammit, she was.

Who would make the first move? Jules didn't know, so she just stood there as the tension in the room ratcheted upward.

Noah lifted one eyebrow, his face hard in the light of the bedside lamp she'd left burning. "You sure about this?" he asked quietly, his lashes dark against his cheek. "Because if we start, I'm not sure that I'll be able to stop."

"I'm sure."

"Then I'm damn grateful."

Noah shrugged out of his jacket, pulled down his tie and tossed both onto the chair, covering her dress with his clothing. Flipping open the button on his collar, he stepped toward her, the pads of his fingers skimming the column of her neck. Her collarbone, the slope of her breast. His gentle touch gave permission for the butterflies in her stomach to lift off. Him taking it slow was more erotic than deep, hot kisses and on-fire hands.

He was such a tough man, so self-contained, but his tenderness was a surprise, his need to draw out their lovemaking astonishing. But he'd speed up in a minute, and they'd go from zero to ballistic. There was too much chemistry between them to allow for a long, slow burn.

Noah held her head in both hands and his thumbs drifted over her eyebrows, down her temples and across her cheekbones.

"Kiss me, No."

Noah half smiled. "Shh. Don't think, don't rush, just feel. Enjoy me loving you. There is no hurry."

Noah didn't wait for or expect a reply, he just lowered his head and his mouth finally—finally!—skimmed hers. As they kissed along slow, heated paths of pleasure, she touched him where she could. She tried to open his shirt with hesitant, shaking fingers, and it seemed like eons passed before she managed to separate the sides of his shirt, allowing her hands to skate across his chest. She pulled her fingers through his chest hair, across his flat nipples, over his rib cage. She dragged her nails over his stomach muscles, feeling like a superhero when he trembled under her touch.

Through the fabric of his pants, she stroked the pad of her finger along his erection, from base to tip, and was rewarded by the sound of a low curse.

Needing more, Jules flipped open the snap on his pants, pulled down his zipper and released his straining erection. Using both hands to cage him, she arched her neck as Noah's mouth headed south, nipping the cords of her neck, sucking on the skin covering the ball of her shoulder.

Without warning, Noah spun her around, ordering her to put her hands on the wall. Following his lead, she gasped when his mouth touched every bump on her spine, barely noticing when her bra fell to the floor at her feet. Stepping close to her, his hands covered her breasts, his thumbs teasing her nipples into hard points.

"I want you," he said, dipping his head to her neck, sucking on that patch of skin where her neck and shoulder met.

Noah hooked his thumbs into her lacy panties and slid them down her legs. Then Noah's hands were on her butt, his fingers sliding between her legs, finding her most sensitive spot with ruthless efficiency. Jules lifted her arms above her head, rested her forehead on her wrists and began to pant.

One finger entered her, then another, and she climbed...reaching, teetering, desperate.

Noah chuckled, pulled his hand away to tease her breasts, slid his fingers across her flat stomach.

"Noah..."

Noah's chest pressed into her back, his erection flirting with her butt. "Yeah?"

"I need—"

"What, babe?"

Jules turned her head and torso and lifted her face, prepared to beg. His eyes, sparking with gold flecks, met hers and then his mouth was over hers, possessive and demanding. Wriggling so that she faced him, Jules hooked a leg over his hip and groaned when his erection brushed her curls, finding her sweet spot.

Pulling her backward, Noah half lifted and half dragged her to her bed, sitting and pulling her down so that her legs fell on either side of his thighs, as close as they could be without him slipping inside.

Noah pushed her hair off her face. "Babe, I need a condom and to get my clothes off. I'm not making love to you half-naked."

Jules moved against him, sliding her core up him. She smiled when Noah's eyes rolled upward. "Okay, in a minute."

Noah gripped her hips and lifted her off him, the muscles in his stomach and arms contracting. *Wow, hot.* Noah stood up, picked up his jacket and found the inside pocket. He pulled out a strip of three condoms, which he tossed onto the bed next to her hip. Jules flopped back on the bed and watched Noah strip, boldly inspecting him from the top of his now-messy hair to his big feet still encased in his shoes. He had a tattoo just above his hip and Jules sat up to take a closer look. After he removed his socks and shoes, she reached for him, allowing her fingers to skate over his ink, a nautical rope.

The knot of the bowline rested on his hip while the rope traveled across the very top of his thigh and onto his lower stomach. Jules appreciated the artist's work, the battered quality suggesting the rope was well used. "Do you miss sailing, No?"

Noah's fingers tunneled into her hair. "Not as much as I missed you."

Not sure how to respond, Jules stared up at him with wide eyes.

Noah pinned her with his gaze, his big body looming over hers. Her legs fell open and his erection nudged her opening. "I need you, Jules. I need to be inside you. To feel... Jesus, Jules."

Jules silently finished his sentence for him: *to feel complete.*

Jules wound her arms around his neck as he slid inside her, just once, skin on skin. Like him, she craved this contact, just for a brief second or maybe a minute, with no emotional or physical barriers. Then Noah pulled out, rolled a condom on and returned to loving her.

Which he did, as he did most things, extremely well.

Nine

Jules...

The next morning, when Jules stepped into her mom's sunny kitchen—Levi's kitchen because it was his house now—Darby grabbed her hand and hopped on one foot.

"Juju! News!"

Jules eyed the full coffeepot. Since Noah spent most of last night doing wonderful things to her that might be illegal in certain countries, she was exhausted. Her brain was fried and her energy levels were low. Speaking of, where was the man of the hour, of the past several hours? Her bed was empty, he wasn't in the bathroom and he wasn't helping Levi make breakfast.

Maybe he wanted to avoid facing her family first

thing in the morning. God knew she did. But it turned out that she needed coffee more than she needed to avoid conversation.

"Guess who had a date last night?" Darby asked, hopping from one foot to the other.

Okay, she and Darby had the twin thing going on, but Darby could *not* know that she'd slept with Noah. No way. Turning her back on her sister, Jules ignored Levi's greeting and grabbed a mug from the cupboard above the coffeepot. Pouring some of the brew into her cup, she took her time turning around, hoping that they wouldn't notice the stubble burn on her jaw and her many-orgasms glow.

"Isn't there a rule in the Bible about talking about this stuff on a Sunday?" Jules asked.

Levi, who was melting butter for—thank you, God— eggs Benedict, glared at Darby. "Don't think so but I wish there was." Levi frowned at her. "Are we talking about you?"

"Me?" Jules slapped her hand on her heart. "Why me?"

She waited for Levi to say that he'd seen Noah walking out of her bedroom but Levi just shook his head and returned to his task of making breakfast.

Dammit. There was nothing to feel embarrassed about. She and Noah were consenting adults, but she didn't feel comfortable with the idea of her brother knowing that she and Noah... Jules shuddered. Too much to handle on little sleep and with no caffeine in her system.

Darby cocked her head. "You look exhausted, Jules. How much sleep did you get last night?"

Not much since she'd spent most of the night exploring the land of Noah. "It's been a long, long week and last night was difficult. Ethan was at Paris's cocktail party and he is going to be the liaison between Paris and Noah, helping her to make decisions about the yacht."

"Dammit," Levi grumbled.

"Why is that a problem?" Darby reached for an apple before jumping up on the kitchen counter, her long legs swinging. "Ethan knows yachts. He taught Noah to sail."

Levi shook his head and turned back to the stove. Jules touched his arm and waited until he looked at her. "How much do you know about their falling-out?"

"Not that much. You know Noah. He's not great at communicating. I've gathered bits and pieces from Eli and Ben, stuff they've said over the years, but I don't know what happened, *exactly*." Levi shook his head. "And I'm not telling you, Jules. It's his story to tell."

His reticence wasn't a surprise. Levi wasn't a gossip.

"I have no idea what's going on," Darby complained, between bites of her apple.

"I'll tell you what I can when I can, Darbs," Jules replied. Wanting to get off the subject of Noah and his past—he'd hate to know they were discussing him—Jules tossed her a smile. "So, what's the big news?"

"Oh, God, gossip." Levi groaned. "Can this wait until later?"

"No." Darby pointed a finger at Levi. "It concerns our mother."

Levi stepped away from the stove and frowned at her. "What's wrong with Mom? Is she hurt? Why aren't you telling me anything?"

Levi went from zero to protective in two seconds flat. Sipping her coffee, Jules eyed her siblings over the rim of her cup.

"She's fine," Darby replied before a sly smile crossed her face. "In fact she's more than fine. I heard that she had a hot date last night. Dancing was involved."

Jules hoped it was with the coffee shop owner. Apart from the fact that he was sexy in an older guy/action hero–type of way, her mom hooking up with him would ensure a decent supply of coffee for a long time to come. Yeah, it wasn't pretty but Jules was willing to encourage this relationship to feed her coffee addiction.

"She went clubbing?" Levi demanded, his expression turning dark.

Go, Mom.

"Where? What? With who?"

Levi looked like he was ready to blow. How could he not know that Darby was winding him up? "Darbs..." she warned.

"Okay, not clubbing. But she did go dancing at a salsa club and she was looking fine."

"How do you know all this?" Levi said, sounding skeptical. Jules shook her head. Darby had friends everywhere and she encouraged those friends to talk, okay, report back to her. She was like the human version of social media.

"A friend of a friend. She also had a dinner date the night before last."

Two guys? Way to go, Mom! Jules grinned but Levi looked like he wanted to rip someone's head off. "Who is he? Where does he work? What does he do? Do we know him? Seriously, I'm going to go over to her house and—"

Jules lifted an eyebrow, waiting to hear what he would do to their mother.

"—give her a stern talking to!" he finished.

Jules giggled. "Calm down, Rambo. She's allowed to have some fun."

"Fun is bowling or golf, not salsa and dinner dates!" Levi picked up some scallions and started chopping the hell out of them.

"Mom is allowed a life. She's been alone a long time. If she wants to get it on, good for her. At least one of us is getting some."

Levi dropped the knife and slapped his hands over his ears. "Shaddup, Darby. Seriously!"

Darby laughed, enjoying Levi's discomfort and her eyes met Jules's, inviting her to share the joke. *Mom's not the only one who is getting lucky...*

Darby heard her silent words and her smile faded, her eyes widening. Jules bit her bottom lip. She normally told Darby everything but she wasn't ready to discuss Noah with her and she wasn't ready to articulate what she was feeling. Mostly because she didn't know what she was feeling, except confused.

Darby glanced at Levi and, seeing that his concentration was back on the scallions, lifted her eyebrows. "Noah?" she mouthed.

Who else? Jules nodded and shook her head. She held up her hand, silently begging her sister to let it go.

Darby pouted before slumping back in her chair, defeated. *We will talk about this.*

I know. Just not yet.

Are you okay?

Yep. Just confused.

Darby waggled her eyebrows. *Tell me this, at the very least. Was he good?*

Jules placed her hand on her heart. *He was amazing.*

"What's going on?"

Jules turned to see DJ standing in the doorway, her eyes bouncing from face to face.

"My mother is salsa dancing and dating two guys. I'm freaking out, and Jules hasn't had any sleep." Levi looked up from his task and pointed his knife at Jules, then Darby. "And Jules and Darby are doing their weird twin, silent communication thing."

DJ placed her hands on her hips, eyed Jules and her sister before turning her attention back to Levi. "Your mom deserves to have some fun, and Jules also, if I'm not mistaken, got herself some last night and that's what they were discussing."

Okay, so it might not just be a twin thing; it might be an I've-known-you-since-you-were-six thing. DJ moved

to stand behind Levi's back and pointed her finger to
the ceiling.

Noah?

Again, who else?

Was it good?

Why were they so concerned about Noah's prowess
in the sack? Seriously?

"I can feel the air moving behind me, DJ," Levi
growled. "Enough already with the sex talk. I don't
want to know who is having sex, when. *Ever,*" Levi
said before sending Jules a hard look. "Do I need to
beat someone up for you?"

Jules quickly shook her head. "No! I'm good." Seeing the concern on Levi's face, she scrambled to find
some words since Levi didn't do the silent communication thing. "I'm good. We're good. Everything is good."

Levi folded his massive arms across his chest.
"Good."

Jules frowned at his sarcastic repetition of her word.

"Because I would hate to have to kick my best
friend's ass. Speaking of, can you find him and tell
him that breakfast will be ready in fifteen?"

Maybe Levi was better at the silent communication
thing than she thought.

As she had a hundred times before but not for a long
time, Jules climbed up the ivy-covered trellis that led up
to what used to be Noah's bedroom within Lockwood
House and wondered what she was doing. She wasn't
ten or fourteen or even eighteen anymore.

A month after Bethann's death, Ethan had closed up the house and moved to the apartment they kept in the city. She remembered hearing her father and mother discussing his abhorrent behavior, his lack of respect, but being young and self-involved, she hadn't paid much attention to their hushed conversations. All she knew was that Noah was hurting and that their family, which had seemed to be rock solid, detonated with Bethann's passing and the reading of the will. Within three months of her death, Noah had left Boston and dropped out of her life.

Why hadn't she pushed and probed, demanded more information? In hindsight, it was easy to see how much Noah was suffering, to see how unhappy he'd been with Morgan, to discern that she wasn't given him the emotional support he needed. Sex with Morgan might've temporarily dulled the pain but sex wouldn't have dulled his grief, his fear.

But Jules knew why she hadn't dug deeper with Noah. She had been upset with him about his involvement with Morgan—jealous, maybe?—and frustrated when he pulled back into his noncommunicative shell. She'd been dealing with her own grief and frustration at not being able to connect with her friend, betrayed by the announcement of his engagement and devastated by his kiss.

Devastated, confused, emotionally battered.

But that was in their past and she had to deal with Noah as he was today, with the adults they both were. He wasn't a young man anymore and she wasn't a teen.

They could, presumably, separate attraction from sex, love from friendship, curtail their wild imaginings...

She was a successful businesswoman, a confident woman...

Who was, technically, trespassing. Jules raised the sash window and flung her leg over the windowsill. Actually, there were no technicalities involved, she was definitely trespassing.

Jules dropped her feet to the floor and wasn't surprised to see Noah in his room, dressed in a pair of old, well-fitting jeans and a long-sleeved gray shirt, the sleeves pushed up to his elbows. Thanks to his recent shower, his blond hair looked a shade darker. She inhaled the dust and mustiness of a closed room but also soap and toothpaste and his special Noah-only scent.

Jules stood up straight, slapped her hands on her butt and looked at Noah. "Levi says breakfast is nearly ready."

Noah sat on the edge of what used to be his bed and frowned at her. "Not that hungry, actually."

Jules wanted to go to him, to drape her arms around his neck and snuggle in, but the expression on his face was remote, his body tense. Knowing that he wouldn't open up without some prodding—if he opened up at all—Jules sat on the edge of the sill and stretched out her legs. "Why did you break into your dad's house, No?"

"Ethan's house," Noah corrected her, his mouth tightening. "He stopped being my dad a decade ago."

"What happened, Noah?"

Noah stared at his feet, his hand draped between

his bent knees. "My mom's will wasn't clear and there was room to maneuver. Ethan essentially tried to screw us out of our inheritance. When he was faced with the choice of inheriting millions or keeping his kids, he chose the cash." Noah stared at the hard, glossy wooden floor. He cleared his throat and when he continued speaking, Jules heard his voice crack with emotion. "He raised us. We called him Dad. Eli and Ben were toddlers when he came into our lives and he spent twenty-plus years being our dad. He was at every sport match he could make, at every play, prize giving. I thought he loved my mom with every fiber of his being.

"Two weeks after her death, I called him at the city apartment and a woman answered his phone, a very young-sounding woman. He was in the shower and she told me that she intended to keep him busy for the rest of the night, if I understood what she meant."

Jules fought the urge to go to him, but if she did he'd clam up and stop talking. She gripped the sill to keep herself in place.

"I confronted Ethan the next day and he laughed in my face. He told me to grow up, that the woman I talked to wasn't the first nor would she be the last. It was what men did, he said."

No, it wasn't. Her dad never cheated on her mom.

Noah's knee bounced up and down. "He then went on to tell me that he'd done his job—he'd raised us as Mom wanted him to do, and he was cashing in. The businesses, the house, the bank accounts, it was payment for being incarcerated in his marriage, his life, for the past twenty years."

Jules bit her lip at Noah's bleak tone. "If I behaved, let him take, well, everything, he'd continue paying for our education, if not, we could waft in the wind."

"Oh, Noah."

"I couldn't let him do that, not without a fight. I needed money to hire lawyers and Ivan gave me more than I needed, provided I stayed engaged to Morgan for two years. After a lot of legal wrangling, the judge gave us the marina and boatyard. Ethan got the cash and the estate. I needed to keep sailing to keep generating the cash to upgrade the marina and boatyard so that they could become profitable again."

"But you did it, Noah. You saved your grandfather's businesses."

Noah lifted his head to look at her. "The price was enormous, Jules. When I finally broke it off with Morgan she had a nervous breakdown and was admitted to some psychiatric facility. They blamed me, despite the fact that our relationship hadn't been anything more than a few calls and emails for months."

"They needed someone to blame, No, and you were handy."

"Maybe." Noah stood up and walked over to his desk, looking at the medals hanging on the wall, the sailing trophies still on the shelf. "Most people think that the opportunity to sail for Wind and Solar was a dream come true."

"Wasn't it?"

She could see the tension in his back in the way he held his neck. But when he turned around and looked at her, Jules saw the devastation on his face. "Leaving Boston was a freaking nightmare. Oh, the sailing was fun, visiting new places was interesting, but when I stepped onto that plane at Logan, I left everything behind. My mom was gone and I was still mourning her, trying to come to terms with her early, brutally unfair death. I lost my dad, too. I didn't recognize the man standing in front of me, taking us to court for *his paycheck.* I had to leave my brothers and hope like hell that they were sensible enough to stay out of trouble, and if not, to run to your folks if they found themselves in a sticky situation. I left my friends, not only Levi, but other friends of both sexes. I left you, the person who knew me best, and I left this weird thing between us, an attraction that blew in from nowhere and was left unexplored. I felt like I had my entire life ripped from me…"

"Which you did." Jules waited a beat before speaking again. "You could've told me this, Noah, at any time. I would've understood because, dammit, I needed to understand."

Noah shrugged. "Time passed and as it did, the words grew harder to say."

Noah pushed his thumbs into his eyes and Jules wondered if it was because he didn't want her to see the tears there. Hers were about to overflow.

Noah folded his arms, looked up at the ceiling and, a long time later, looked back. The grief was gone and determination was back on his face. "There is no way

I am going back there, Jules, back to that place where I felt lost and scared and alone. I've learned how to live on my own, be on my own—I can't do this happy-family thing…"

She didn't recall asking him to but…okay.

Noah looked around the room, his face hard. "This is just a house, these are just things. This is just land. My mom isn't here and by buying it I won't change the past, change what he did, the choices I made. Mom doesn't care whether it stays in the family or not—she's not here!"

Jules winced at the muted roar. "I'm killing myself, and for what? To design a boat for a woman who doesn't seem to care what I come up with or not? So that I can raise the money to buy a property I'm not sure I even want in a town that holds nothing but bad memories for me?"

Well, that stung.

"I could forget about buying the house and the estate. I could walk away. I have a client begging me to meet him on the Costa Smeralda, another in Hawaii, both wanting designs I could do in my sleep. I don't need to be here, Jules! I don't need this crap in my life! Sun, sailing and sex…with none of the drama!"

Jules nodded, pain punching tiny holes in her stomach lining and her heart. He didn't want a life in Boston and he didn't want her. He needed his freedom, she knew this… She'd always known this. So why did it hurt so much? Jules pushed her hair off her face and forced herself to look him in the eye, to confront her feelings.

"I'm sorry you feel like that, No. I'm sorry that you think a life in Boston can't give you what you need."

"You don't know what I need, Jules!"

Yeah, she did, but getting him to realize that was an impossibility. But she'd try. At least once... "You need us, Noah, and you need *me*. You need to wake up with someone who loves you, who gets you, understands your past and who will always be on your side. You need to spend your days with your brothers and play pool with them in The Tavern and golf outside your front door. You need to have coffee and dinner with my mom and talk about your mom. You need to buy this house and you need to *stay*."

Noah frowned at her and she could see hope and frustration and fear going to war in his eyes. "Why do you say that?"

Because she loved him. She'd loved him every day of her life and she'd fallen in love with him again when she saw him standing naked in her shower. Her brain had just needed a little time to come to terms with what her heart always knew.

"Because if you walk away from this house, from Boston, from me, you're going to regret it every day for the rest of your life. You belong here, Noah. You belong with me."

Jules held up her hand, knowing he was about to make a hard rebuttal. "I get it, Noah. I understand how much it must have hurt leaving because I felt it, too. Not having you in my life was horrendous and I was determined that I wouldn't give you another chance to hurt me. But here I am, doing it again. Love is scary, Noah, but it's the one thing that should be scary! We shouldn't just be able to jump into love without thought. I know if you walk away again I'll be in a world of pain, *again*, but I can't divorce myself from what I feel because loving you is an essential part of who I am."

Jules stood up and made herself smile as she placed one leg over the windowsill. "If you leave, if you don't fight for this house, fight for your life, fight for me, you'll be an old man living with regret, unable to look yourself in the eye."

"I don't love you, Jules."

Such impetuous, defiant words. Jules closed her eyes, trying to hold back the pain. "Of course you love me, Noah. You always have. Just as I've always loved you. You're just too damn scared to admit it and even more terrified to do something about it."

Callie...

There was no way that Mason would hear that she'd been on two dates in the past week. While many of her friends frequented his coffee shop, she doubted that he made it a habit to quiz the elderly about their love lives.

And if he did, he shouldn't.

Her friends, the few who knew she was dating, wouldn't think to tell him. To them Mason was part of the service industry, not someone to gossip with. The thought made her feel ugly, petty and ashamed. She shouldn't even be coming here but she was as addicted to his gorgeous face as she was to his coffee blend.

Oh, who was she kidding? He could serve strychnine-flavored java and she'd be coming back for more. It was official: she was pathetic. Callie pushed open the door to the coffeehouse and cursed when her eyes flew around the room, instinctively seeking out the man she'd come to see. She'd blown off a round of golf this morning with Patrick and an invite to lunch with John. Her dates thought that their evenings had gone well but, apart from the salsa dancing, she'd been as bored as hell—and Mason was to blame.

Patrick and John were perfectly nice, urbane, successful men in their early sixties. Accomplished, successful and courteous, they were appropriate men for a woman of her age to date.

They were also deeply, fundamentally, jaw-breakingly boring. And they seemed, dammit, old.

"Stop frowning. You're going to get wrinkles," Mason murmured.

Callie turned her head to see him standing behind her, dressed in khaki shorts and an untucked, white button-down shirt with the cuffs rolled back. He was carrying a cup of coffee and a slice of carrot cake, and her mouth watered—at the sight of him and the dessert. She couldn't indulge; she had to try and keep her muffin top under some sort of control. Though she suspected that horse had bolted a long, long time ago...

"I already have wrinkles," Callie told him, sitting down at the nearest table and glaring at him.

"Hardly any," Mason replied, his eyes wandering over her face and down her neck. "In fact, you have the most gorgeous skin. Want some coffee?"

No, I want to stop thinking about you. I want to stop imagining what your hands feel like on my skin, your tongue in my mouth. I want to be able to date and not feel like I am cheating on my dead husband and you.

Callie sighed. "S'pose."

Mason delivered the coffee and carrot cake to a nearby table before returning to her side. He held her chin and lifted her head, blue eyes assessing. "Who pissed on your battery?"

He was so damn irreverent. "Don't be crude."

Mason's thumb skimmed her bottom lip. "Stop acting like you are 103. Spit it out, woman."

She should object to him calling her "woman," should tell him to go to hell. But his rough voice and the tenderness in his eyes just warmed her from the inside out.

Or more accurately, from that space between her legs and up.

Callie gestured for him to take the other seat. "Don't call me 'woman,' and don't loom over me. Sit if you want to but don't...*hover*."

Mason frowned, slid into the chair opposite her and rested his arms on the table. He didn't speak. He just looked at her with assessing eyes. Callie drummed her fingers on the table between them, wondering what to say. She couldn't tell him that she'd missed him, that she'd wanted to be with him, that eating out with another man seemed wrong.

"Cal? Talk to me."

"Jules, my daughter, is going through a rough time. She and the man she loves, who I think also loves her, can't find a way to be together."

Mason remained silent for a moment. "As a parent, I fully understand that you are worried but that's not why you are upset. Tell me the truth, the full truth." Mason stopped one of his passing waitresses, ordered a latte and turned his attention back to her.

"I wanted an espresso," Callie muttered.

"No, you didn't, and aren't I supposed to be the child in this nonrelationship?" Mason asked, his voice sounding tougher than she'd ever heard it. Callie flushed, sat back and tried to get her anger under control. None of this was his fault and her acting like an angry teenager wasn't helping.

"One of the reasons I like you, Callie, is that you appear to be a straight shooter. So, last chance, speak or shut up," Mason said, his eyes flat and his jaw hard.

Callie ran her thumbnail across the wooden table. "I went on two dates this past week."

Mason immediately stiffened. "Why are you telling me this?"

"Because they were very nice, very successful men of a certain age and they were—"

"I think I'm going to throw up," Mason interjected.

"—as boring as hell. I spent most of that time wishing they were you," Callie continued, ignoring him.

Mason's eyes lightened, darkened and lightened again. Callie fell into all that interest and emotion and, yeah, desire. "What are you saying, Callie?"

"I'm saying that I am a fifty-four-year-old woman who is not only just coming out of mourning, but menopause, too. I am a cocktail of hormones, insecurity and confusion. I am both terrified of having sex and equally terrified of not ever having it again. I've been a wife, am still sort of a mommy, but I've forgotten how to be a woman."

Mason ran his hand over his jaw, visibly shocked by her blunt speech.

"I want you but I don't want to want you. I don't want to disappoint you but I don't want to disappoint myself. I'm never getting married again—Ray was the only husband I'll ever have."

"Jesus."

If she stopped now, she'd never start again. "If you keep asking me, I might say yes to a date. I might even get up enough courage to put my overweight, very unsexy body in your hands and I might let you kiss me."

"*Might?* Screw that."

Mason pulled her to her feet and led her through the crowded tables toward the counter on the far side of the room. Callie tried to tug her hand away but he was too strong and, yeah, this was the most excitement she'd had since she and Ray made love in the hot tub—

The slap of Mason's hand on a swinging door dragged her from that memory—from the guilt rising in her—and she found herself in a tiny kitchen.

Mason hauled her across the room and, keeping his hand around her wrist, flipped the dead bolt on the back door. Hot, humid air swirled around her as Mason guided her down the steps and, the next moment, her back was against the rough brick wall. Mason stared down at her, his eyes boring into her.

"Tell me now you don't want this and I'll back off."

Callie placed her hands on his chest and lifted her face up. "I do but I shouldn't—"

"Again, screw that."

Mason's hands captured her face and his mouth covered hers and plundered, sliding over hers like he owned it, his tongue twisting hers into submission.

This wasn't a boy's kiss but a man's, a man who knew what he wanted and how he intended to get it. There was no hesitation because Mason listened to her body language, saw the desire in her eyes. Impatient and determined, he wasn't the type to waste time, to hang around waiting for her to be 100 percent ready.

Turned out that he was right, she was ready. Her tongue knew what to do, her hands ran up his strong back, down his hard butt, skirted around to feel his flat, hard stomach. Since she was touching him, Mason obviously thought that a little quid pro quo was in order and his broad hand sneaked between them and covered her breast, immediately finding her nipple and rubbing it into a hard, tight point.

It felt natural to tilt her pelvis, to push against that long, hard erection...

His erection. His...

Erection.

God, she was kissing a man who wasn't her husband, who was so much younger than her, in the alley behind his coffeehouse. *Whoa, brakes on, Brogan.*

Mason, feeling her resistance, rested his forehead on hers. "Please don't regret this, Callie. You didn't do anything wrong."

Callie's hands fell to her sides as Ray's face flashed on the big screen in her mind. What would he think? What would her kids think? Her friends? Callie stepped away from Mason, who looked flushed and, oh, so frustrated.

"Then why do I feel like I have?"

"This again." Mason shoved his hands into his hair. "He's dead, Callie, and you're alive, still here, still sexy, still a woman. You didn't die with him."

"A part of me did, Mason!" Callie cried. "And the part of me that is waking up is still coming to terms with all of this!"

Mason's eyes flashed with irritation. "I'm not going to beg, Callie. Or run after you. Or wait forever."

Callie narrowed her eyes, suddenly furious. "That's such a man thing to say! Because it's not going your way, you issue a threat? Guess what, Mason? I'm not young enough or stupid enough or insecure enough to fall for that BS!

"This goes at my pace or it doesn't go at all," Callie added, furious.

Callie saw the regret in his eyes, the apology hovering on his lips. It had been a spur-of-the-moment statement, something she instinctively knew he regretted, but it gave her a damn good excuse to walk away, to put a whole lot of daylight and space between her and this man who'd dropped into her life and flipped it upside down.

"I'm not going to come back here for a while. I need time to think," Callie told him.

Mason nodded, clearly still frustrated but back in control. He gestured at the still-open door. "I'll follow you in shortly. I need some time."

"For what?" Callie asked the question without thinking and frowned at his raised eyebrows. Then Mason shocked her by grabbing her hand and placing her palm on his very hard penis. Through his shorts she could feel his strength, the sheer masculinity under her palm. She leaned forward, wanting to kiss him but Mason pulled back and dropped her hand.

He turned away, and when he spoke his voice sounded rough. And a little sad. "Go inside, Callie. I'll see you when and if I see you."

Walk away, Brogan. It was the right thing to do. She didn't want to, but Callie forced herself to pull open the door to the coffee shop, to step back into the cool kitchen.

Back to reality, where it was safe. But where it was also so damn lonely.

And brutally unexciting.

Ten

Noah...

Of course you love me, Noah, you always have. Just as I've always loved you. You're just too damn scared to admit it and even more terrified to do something about it.

Jules's words rolled around Noah's head as they had every minute for the past three weeks. He wanted to dismiss them, to shrug them off as a figment of her over-active imagination, but they ran across his mind on a never-ending ticker tape.

He wanted her, of course he did, she was everything he wanted, but he was too damn scared, comprehensively terrified of what it meant to go all in with Jules.

Noah thought that he had just cause to be. He'd had everything at one point in his life; he'd had the world at his feet. A solid family structure, parents who adored him, pain-in-the-ass brothers who'd charge hell if he needed them to. Friends—good, close friends.

Then, like a cheap car slamming into the back of a heavy rig at high speed, his life had crumpled and crashed around him and his world as he knew it ended. Everything he knew, relied upon, was no longer there. The people he thought he knew morphed into strangers. His dad became his enemy, his girlfriend a means to an end, his friendship with Jules suddenly colored by a shocking dose of lust. Leaving his life behind hadn't been a choice. But walking away still hurt like the hot, sour bite of hell.

He didn't think he could cope with loving something— a person, his life, normality—and having it ripped from him again. But nor could he live a life that didn't have Jules in it. And he didn't want her as his friend...

Rock and hard place, meet the devil and the deep blue sea.

He loved her, of course he did. He'd loved the ten-year-old Jules who caught frogs and climbed trees, the fourteen-year-old with braces, the young woman he'd watched evolve into an adult woman. Then he kissed her and he saw a thousand galaxies in her eyes, felt the power of the universe in her touch. That hadn't changed: Jules was still, and always would be, the person who made his world turn.

Tides changed, the moon waxed and waned, and seas

dipped and rose but Jules was his sextant, his North Star, his GPS.

Wherever she was, was where he wanted to be. But fear, cold and hard, still gripped his heart. God, he'd much rather be fighting a squall in the Southern Ocean than be caught in this emotional maelstrom.

Noah looked up at the rap on his door frame, happy for any distraction coming his way. Levi stood in the doorway, dressed in board shorts and dock shoes, his red T-shirt faded by sunlight. Noah noticed the six-pack in his hand, the bottles dripping with condensation. Hell, yes, he could do with one or three of those.

Levi walked into his office, tossed him a beer and sat down on his chair, his long legs stretched out in front of him. Noah cracked the top, took a long sip and rested the cold bottle on his aching head. "So, you need to make a formal offer on the Lockwood Trust in two days or the estate will go on the market," Levi said bluntly.

He was aware. "There's no chance Paris will sign the final design by then. Ethan won't let her."

"Has Jules completed her designs?"

Noah glanced at the folder holding Jules's sketches, the fabric samples, the wonderful mock-ups of the yacht's interiors. They'd been communicating via email for weeks but Jules still managed to do a stunning job and Paris, and anyone with taste, would love her designs. "She's done. So am I. Paris just needs to approve the designs."

"So when are you meeting her?"

"I haven't made an appointment to see her yet." Levi pulled a face and Noah shook his head at his friend's disapproval. "I know I should but I keep wondering what's the point? Ethan will shoot down everything I say, he'll demand a redesign and time will run out. I've been working on other projects but my fees won't earn anywhere near as much as what Paris cane pay me. Basically, I'm screwed."

Levi frowned before pointing the top of his bottle in Noah's direction. "Sorry, who are you and what have you done with Noah Lockwood?"

Noah sent him a blank look, wondering if Levi had had a few more beers before ending up in his office.

"Noah, one of the things that set you apart from other sailors was your utter belief in yourself and the course you were on. You backed yourself a hundred percent and you never ever gave up. Where's that dude?"

Noah opened his mouth to blast Levi, to defend himself, but Levi spoke over him. "You always raced until the bitter end, sometimes you went across the finish line without realizing that you were done, that you had won the race, because you were so damn focused, because you fought, right up until the end. You still have a couple of days. Why the hell aren't you still fighting?"

"I…uh…" Crap, he didn't have an answer for that.

"My sister—the miserable one living in my house—and your future are deserving of all your effort, Noah, all your competitive spirit and every last bit of determination," Levi said, emotion bleeding through his tough words. He leaned forward, his intense gaze nailing Noah to his chair. "It's the Rolex Sydney Hobart Yacht Race, you and your closest competitor are in the Bass Strait and it's neck and neck. Are you going to alter course, or are you going to hold your nerve, and your course, and fight for the win?"

Adrenaline pumped through his system. He could taste the drops of seawater on his lips, the wind blowing in his hair. Wind catching his sails, he could hear the whoop of his teammates as his yacht sailed forward.

Keeping his eyes on Levi's, he drained his beer and reached for his phone. "I'm going to hold my course."

Levi nodded and the fire of frustration in his eyes died. "Thank God, I wasn't looking forward to kicking your ass."

For the first time in days, Noah smiled. "As if you could. Now, get lost. I've got a house to buy and a meeting to set up."

Levi ambled to his feet, snagging the plastic cage holding the beers. "And a girl to win?"

"Yeah. And a girl to win."

Levi looked concerned. "And if you lose?"

Noah lifted one shoulder and held his friend's eye. "I never lose, Levi. But there's a first time for everything and if that happens, I'll do what I always do..."

"And that is?"

"Stand in the storm, ride it out and keep adjusting my sails."

Jules...

I am not going to cry. That will not happen. This is business. Paris is a client and Noah is a colleague. You can do this. You have to do this.

Woman up, Brogan.

Jules placed her hand on the wall next to the elevator in the lobby of Paris's building and stared at the expensive marble flooring. Dammit, this hurt. Every cell in her body ached, her eyes were red rimmed from crying too many tears and from nights without sleep. She felt sick from the tips of her toes to her ears. God, even her hair hurt. She was fundamentally, utterly miserable.

Her fault, so her fault. She told herself not to fall for Noah again, she knew a broken heart was a possibility. Heartbreak, such small words for such a life-altering condition. Jules wished she could go back to her childhood, when skinned knees and broken arms hurt and were inconvenient but they healed, dammit. This…this gut-ripping, soul-mincing pain was going to be with her for a long, long time. And she knew she'd never be the same person again, she was irrevocably changed. Quieter, harder, a lot more lost and very alone.

This was now her life.

Jules looked down at the screen on her phone and glared at the prosaic, to-the-point message on her screen. Five o'clock meeting with Paris. Be there.

Noah's terse instructions were followed by Paris's address.

Jules hadn't spoken to Noah since leaving him in his

childhood bedroom nearly a month ago. He didn't come back to the house for breakfast, and when he didn't contact her on Monday, or on any day that following week, she assumed that history was repeating itself and Noah was retreating from her bed and her life. She spent every moment she had working on her designs for the yacht—the sooner she finished with them, the sooner this would all be over—and couriered the finished designs and the sketches to Noah's office two weeks ago.

She'd yet to hear whether he approved, what he thought. She could be going into a presentation showing Paris sketches and designs Noah hated. Because she still had her pride, and that meant that she had a reputation to maintain, a job to complete and that meant—*grrr*—obeying his text message order. She'd never bailed on a project and didn't intend to now. No matter how difficult it would be to see Noah again, knowing he chose his fear over her, she would get into this damn elevator and finish the job.

If she didn't, she would never be able to look herself in the eye again. *Time to be brave, Brogan.* An hour, maybe more, and she'd be done. She could go home, pull a blanket over her head and shut out the world. And release all the tears that were gathering in her throat.

Jules left the elevator and walked down the long hallway, telling herself that this was it, this was the last time she would be seeing Noah for God knew how long. Standing outside Paris's door, she worked her fist into her sternum, mentally tossing water on the fire in her stomach.

*An hour, Brogan. You can do this. You have no
choice!*

Wishing she was anywhere else—she was exhausted
and stressed and *sad*, dammit—Jules knocked on Paris's
door and jumped when the door swung open. Noah stood
there, strong and confident in his gray suit, white shirt
and scarlet power tie. His hair was brushed off his forehead and he looked like he could stroll into any business
meeting anywhere in the world and take control.

Jules met his eyes and frowned at the tenderness she
saw within those brown depths, the flicker of amusement. He thought this was funny? His inheritance was
on the line and her heart was hemorrhaging, and he
was amused? Jules welcomed the surge of anger and
clenched her fists, the urge to smack him almost overwhelming.

She hauled in a breath, then another, knowing that
her face reflected all her suppressed rage. She was going
to kill him, slowly and right there. A sympathetic female
judge would understand, she was sure of it.

"You look like you are about to blow a gasket."

A gasket, an engine, input the codes to set off a nuclear strike. How dare he stand there looking rested and
relaxed? Did he have any idea of the strolls she'd taken
through hell lately?

"I— You— I'm… God!" Jules rubbed her fingers
across her forehead. She couldn't do this, there was no
chance. She was leaving, going home and crawling into
bed before she fell apart completely. She wasn't brave
and she definitely wasn't strong.

"I've got to go." Jules managed to whisper the words and turned to leave. Noah's hand on her arm pulled her back to face him, and then his hands were on her hips and drawing her slowly and deliberately toward himself. When not even an ant could crawl between them, he brushed his mouth across hers, his tongue tracing the seam of her lips, before lifting his head.

Why was he doing this? Was he trying to torture her?

No more. She was done with this. Jules slid her fingers under his open suit jacket, grabbed the skin at his waist and gave it a hard twist.

Noah's eyes widened and she heard his pained gasp. "Ow. For what?"

"Do you know how much it hurts to kiss you, knowing that I might never be able to do that again?" Jules hissed, furious at the tears that clouded her vision. "That's not fair, Noah, and worse than that, it's cruel."

Noah rubbed the back of his neck, looking shocked and a little embarrassed. "Jules, babe, just hang on."

"For what, Noah? No, I'm done! I can't do this anymore. It hurts too damn much!"

Noah touched her cheek with his knuckle. "I'm asking you, one more time, to trust me. Please, Jules."

Jules shook her head, willing away the tears in her eyes. "I don't think I can, Noah. You've drained me of the little strength I had left."

"Dammit, Jules—"

"Julia? Oh, is Julia here?" Paris trilled from somewhere in the cavernous apartment behind them. "Noah!

Is that Julia? If it is, tell her to come and have a glass of champagne and to show me her pretty, pretty work."

Jules closed her eyes, twisted her lips and, refusing to look at the man she wanted the most but couldn't have, turned on her heel and forced herself to walk into Paris's luxurious apartment.

Noah...

Noah was regarded as one of the best sailors of his generation, one of the top money earners in the sport. He was a decent businessman, successful and wealthy. A good brother and friend. None of that meant anything, everything was stripped away, and he was now just the man who'd made Jules cry.

Never again. He was done with that. From this moment on, Jules and her happiness were his highest priority, making sure that she'd never have cause to doubt him again, his lifetime goal. And, because he didn't want her to suffer longer than she had to, Noah injected steel into his spine and followed his woman into the overly decorated lounge of Paris's apartment.

Ethan was at the meeting, just as he'd expected and banked on him to be. Noah had given their encounter a lot of thought so he had a plan. Taking control of the presentation—knowing that Jules needed something to anchor her—he suggested a virtual tour of the yacht. He quickly connected his laptop to Paris's big-screen TV and, thanks to some very high-tech computer software, showed Paris what he and Jules envisaged for the yacht, inside and out. Pity their client couldn't feel the waves rolling under the hull, taste the salt on her lips, but that being said, it was still kick-ass tech.

As he'd requested, Paris and Ethan kept their comments until the end, allowing him and Jules to complete their presentation before they were bombarded with questions.

"It's beautiful." Paris sighed and clasped her hands. "Utterly marvelous. What shall I call her?"

"Whatever you like." Noah smiled but it faded when he darted a glance at Jules and saw her blank face.

"Before your rhapsodizing gets out of control, my dear, I should like to point out that there are some very crucial design flaws in what Noah has presented," Ethan said, his voice pitched low. No, there weren't. How could Paris not hear the malice in his voice, see the spite in his eyes?

And so it started.

Placing his ankle on his knee, Noah cocked his head. Ethan met his eyes, not for one minute believing that Noah would rake up the past. It was a fair conclusion for him to reach; generally, Noah would rather bleed to death before asking for a bandage, help or even a plaster. Well, not this time. There was too much at stake.

"There are no flaws in the design," Noah said, his voice calm. "Ethan is just saying that to irritate me."

Paris frowned. "Nonsense! He's your stepfather. He raised you. And he's just trying to make your design better and to look after my interests."

Noah shook his head, conscious of Jules's eyes on

his face. "Ethan never looks after anyone's interests but his own, Paris. He doesn't want you to sign off on the design, because if you do that, then he has to sell Lockwood Estate to me, at twenty percent below the market price. He'd lose twenty million if that happens."

"That's not true," Ethan bit out, turning an alarming shade of red.

Noah dropped his leg, leaned forward and opened a folder, pulling out a copy of the judgment. He pushed it across the table in Paris's direction. "Proof." Noah reached across the table and took Paris's hand in his. Damn, he didn't want to hurt her but when it came to choosing between her happiness and Jules's, between saving his inheritance and kicking Ethan out of his life forever, he would. Besides, she and Ethan had only been together a few weeks; she was as much a victim of his machinations as he was.

"Paris, I like you. You're a pain in the ass to work for, but you have a warm heart, a romantic heart. I think you are wonderfully charming and witty but you *are* a woman of a certain age."

Paris narrowed her eyes at that statement and Noah ignored her, along with Ethan's growls of disapproval. Noah forced himself to articulate the words. "Ethan doesn't date woman your age, in fact he rarely dates anyone over the age of twenty-five." *Dammit, just spit it out!* "The only reason he's dating you is because you are rich and he's broke."

"I am not! This is slander! How dare you?"

"Noah—"

Noah ignored Jules's quiet warning and flicked a quick glance at Ethan, looking apoplectic with rage. He pulled out another stack of papers and put them in front of Paris. "Photos of his last ten girlfriends, copies of his credit report—he owes money all around town."

Paris looked down, flicked through the papers and when she lifted her head again, her eyes were flint hard. *Gotcha, you bastard.*

"Those are bogus—you can't prove anything. Paris, it's not true. He's been lying to you, too… He and Jules aren't romantically involved, he just said it to appeal to your softer side," Ethan shouted.

Noah cursed when doubt flew into Paris's eyes. Deliberately not looking at Jules, he held Paris's gaze and waited for the question. If she didn't believe him, he was sunk. He'd lose the house, his time and the money.

He could live with losing all three but, God, if he lost Jules…

"Are you and Jules not romantically involved?"

Noah had to answer her honestly, knowing that nothing else but the truth would get him through this quagmire. "There's nothing romantic about Jules and I," he replied, sighing when he heard the harsh note in his own voice and Jules's gasp.

Okay, not off to a good start. He rubbed his hand over his head, ordering his tongue to cooperate. "*Romance* implies something ephemeral, wishy-washy, fleeting. Jules and I have known each other too long and too well to settle for such a weak description of our relationship."

Paris tipped her head to the side. "So how would you characterize it?"

Well, hell, he was going to have to say it after all. And with an audience. Okay, then. Noah shifted his gaze from Paris's face to Jules's, her light eyes surprised and, yes, terrified.

Join the freakin' club.

"She's been my best friend all my life, my rock, my true north. She's the reason the moon pulls the tide, why the earth spins, the reason my sun sets and falls.

"Yes, we started off by faking something that we thought wasn't there, not knowing that it was, that it has always been a part of me, of us."

Jules clasped her hands together, her face devoid of color, her eyes begging for more. Something to banish the last of her fear, something that would restore her trust. Noah kept his eyes on her face but directed his words at Paris. "Sign off on the yacht or don't, Paris. Yeah, a part of me will be sad at missing out on reclaiming the house and land that's been in my family for generations, but I'll live with it. What I can't live without, what I refuse to live without, is Jules. I'd live in a freakin' cardboard box if it meant being with her. She's my…" His voice broke when he saw the tears in Jules's eyes. He swallowed and bit the flesh on the inside of his cheek to keep it together. Were her tears a good sign? Bad? He couldn't tell.

He forced himself to speak again, this time speaking to Jules directly. "You're…everything, Jules. You always will be, I promise."

Jules lifted her fist to her mouth, the tears now running down her face. What did they mean? Did he still have a chance? God, he hoped so. When they were alone he'd drag more out of her. Things like "Yes, let's give us a chance" or "Okay, we can go out on a date." He was intelligent enough to know that he'd hurt her—again— and that she'd take her time forgiving him, that she'd have to learn to trust him all over again.

He could live with that. After all, he wasn't going anywhere for a while and when he did he was coming straight back to Boston.

Paris cleared her throat, pushed the stack of papers incriminating Ethan away from her. "Out."

Noah thought she was talking to him but then realized that she was looking at Ethan. "You have a minute to leave my home. If you do not do so in that time, I will not only have you ostracized from polite society, I will tell every rich young lady I come across that you have impotence issues."

Noah turned to smile at Jules and his breath hitched at the flicker of hope he saw in her eyes. He pushed his chair back, intending to go to her, to pull her into his arms, when Paris gripped his wrist. Her fingernails pushed into his skin. "Oh, no, you don't. You are going to keep your hands off her until we've gone through your design in detail. Then I'll sign off on the design and write you a check."

Noah groaned, Jules whimpered and Paris looked from him to Jules and back to him, resignation in her eyes. "Oh, all right, then! Contract signing and check but I'll expect you both back here tomorrow to talk about my beautiful, beautiful yacht. Will you two have sorted yourselves out by then?"

Noah, still unsure, darted a glance at Jules, who had yet to speak. "Hopefully."

Jules pulled a tissue out of her bag, wiped her eyes and hauled in a breath. Then her eyes focused and she nodded at the folder in front of him. "Let's get this done, Noah."

So, what did that mean? And where the hell did he stand?

Jules...

Noah decided that the closest place they could find privacy was on the *Resilience*, and unlike what happened in movies, they didn't run down the sidewalks of Boston, pushing past people to get to the marina. Silently, they took the elevator to the ground floor, where they caught a taxi to the marina. At the access gate, Noah plugged in his code, escorted Jules through the turnstile and to the far quay where his magnificent J-class yacht was berthed, her tall mast making her easily recognizable.

It felt like she was having an out-of-body experience— had Noah really told her, in front of people, that he loved her? It was so surreal, like it was the best dream ever. God, she really hoped she never woke up. Jules slipped off her shoes, sighing when her bare feet hit the teak deck. She headed to the bow, where she sank down and dangled her feet off the edge of the yacht.

Jules lifted her head and saw Noah looming over her, looking unsure. She patted the space next to her and Noah shrugged out of his jacket, pulled off his tie and dropped them to the warm deck, immediately lifting his face to the sun.

"Did you mean it?" Jules asked quietly, searching his eyes for the truth.

Because he knew her so well, he didn't need clarification on exactly what she was asking. He nodded. "Absolutely." Noah flipped open the cuffs on his shirt and started to roll them up. "You were right, you know. About me loving you, that I always have."

She could barely hear his precious words over the sound of her own heartbeat... Dare she believe this was really happening?

Noah managed a smile, his eyes intense as he tucked a strand of hair behind her ear. Immediately the wind blew it across her mouth again.

"Do you...love me? Back at Lockwood House, you told me you did but that could've changed in the last three weeks."

She saw his fear of being rejected and her heart lurched. This was Noah as she'd never seen him before: humbled, vulnerable, uncertain. *This mattered, she mattered*.

Jules touched his cheek, ran her hands over his thin lips. "My first memory was you picking me up when I fell. I think Darby pushed me off the swing. You helped me up and I looked at you and I felt...whole. My three-year-old heart recognized you... I'm not putting this well." Jules stumbled over her words. "I've spent the last ten years looking for something I always had, something that I only feel when I'm with you. You are what I need in my life, No, the only thing I need. It's more than love. It's..."

Noah finally smiled at her. "Right."

Yeah, it was. Being with Noah was where she was supposed to be, being his was what she was meant to do. They had their careers and their interests and their friends, but they were destined to be a unit. She and Darby might've shared a womb but she was convinced she and Noah shared a heart.

Noah's mouth skimmed hers but he pulled back when desire flared. "Can we do this? Be together?"

"We can do anything, No. Yeah, your work is mostly overseas but we can work around that." It would be hard but he was worth it. He was worth *everything*.

"My client consults are overseas. My work doesn't have to be. Technology pretty much allows me to work anywhere, and most of my correspondence with my freelance staff is done online. I'd still have to travel but I could easily make my base here in Boston."

"Is this where you want to be?" Jules asked him, unable to disguise the tremor and hope in her voice.

"Jules, you are where I want to be," Noah replied, sounding confident again. "Your business is here, your clients are here. If I want to be with you, and I do, then Boston is where I'll be." He held up his hand when she opened her mouth to speak. "And, yeah, of course I'm moving here to be with you but, as you pointed out, my brothers are here, Levi, my businesses. Added bonuses."

The sun was shining, the air was fresh but her lungs felt constricted; she couldn't breathe. This was her fantasy, the best news she could get and she was on the verge of passing out. The cliché about being careful what you wish for drifted through her head.

Jules sucked in some air, waited for her head to clear, before using both hands to hold back her hair. She wanted to look at Noah, see his eyes when she asked him her next question, the one she had to have an answer for.

"Can I trust you? Will you promise not to wander off with my heart again?"

Noah scooted closer to her, his hand covering the side of her face. "My heart is yours, babe. It always has been. You know that."

"As mine is yours," Jules said.

Noah pushed a curl behind her ear. "I need to go to Costa Smeralda to meet with an oil sheikh who wants me to design a state-of-the-art yacht. No longer content to have oil wells and hotels and race horses, he now wants to sail competitively. I thought you could come with me and we could have a preengagement honeymoon."

Jules's mouth curved. "So, we are getting married?"

Noah's mouth slid across hers in a kiss that promised her forever. "Damn right we are. But right now you need to kiss me."

So Jules did. In fact, they kissed for so long and with

so much abandon that numerous complaints were laid at the receptionist's desk against the couple who were, as one elderly sailor stated, "oblivious to the world."

It took a minute of Levi calling their names and one shrill whistle to pull them apart.

"Get a room!" Levi told them, looking up at them when they peered over the hull of the boat. Their dopey, radiant faces told him everything he needed to know.

"Lee, we've decided to get married!" Jules shouted, incandescently happy.

Levi placed his hands on his hips and smiled. "Honey, that decision was made for you twenty-plus years ago by Mom and Bethann. You've just taken your time to get with the program."

Jules and Noah exchanged broad smiles. It was probably true but neither of them minded.

"Congrats, guys. But enough public displays of affection, okay?" Levi asked. *"Please?"*

Jules laughed, shook her head and looked at Noah as Levi turned away. "Love you, Noah." She couldn't say it enough, she had ten years of lost time to make up for.

"I love you more, babe. So, do you want to go belowdecks?" Noah said as he stood up, holding out his hand.

Jules placed her hand in his and allowed him to pull her up and into his chest. Yes, of course she did. On land or sea, being with him was the only place she wanted to be.

Epilogue

Callie...

One down, four to go, Callie thought, thinking of the call she'd received from Jules an hour earlier. She stood in front of the front door to Mason's coffee shop, frowning at the closed sign. It was after five; Mason closed at four thirty and he'd already be on his way home.

It was better that he was gone, she wasn't even sure why she was there. Callie rested her hand on the cool glass and remembered feeling and sounding as giddy as Jules did when she and Ray announced that they were in love, that they were getting married. It was all so new; she'd been a virgin, he'd only had one other lover. They were each other's first loves, their *only* loves. She didn't know how to love anyone but Ray and didn't think she could.

He'd been a wonderful husband, a considerate lover, an excellent father. They'd traveled, raised their kids, socialized. And she still loved him with every breath she took. He'd been her world, still was. Oh, she'd been to grief counseling and knew she could be idealizing Ray and their relationship, it was what everyone did. But they'd had fun, dammit, and it was as good as she remembered.

Her attraction to Mason, the crazy, heat-filled dreams, her fantasies of his broad hands on her skin, touching her in the places that only Ray knew, filled her with guilt and she felt like she was cheating on her husband. Her lust for this younger, *hotter* guy was tearing her in two.

And the affection she was feeling, the connection that arced between them, burned a hole in her stomach. She had no right to feel this way, to be both terrified and excited at seeing Mason…as well as annoyed and irritated and turned on. Even in those early days with Ray their attraction hadn't burned so brightly. It had been a steady flame instead of a bonfire.

She loved her husband, she *did*. So why, when she was supposed to be so happy for her daughter, so excited for her future, couldn't she stop thinking about this denim-blue-eyed man? Why could she still taste him in her mouth, feel his hand on her breast? Why did she ache between her legs?

And, this made her blood run cold, what compelled

her to run to him, oh, so desperately wanting to share her wonderful news? Why was he the first person she wanted to tell?

It couldn't work, it would never work. She was Callie Brogan, still in love with her husband and Mason was the coffee shop guy.

The door under her hand moved and Callie lifted up her tear-soaked face, her eyes colliding with his. His hand encircled her wrist and he gently pulled her into the empty shop, chairs on tables, a mop and bucket in the center of the floor. He wiped away her tears with his thumb before gently pulling her into his arms, his hand holding the back of her head.

"Hey, honey, what's the matter, huh? What can I do?"

"Nothing. Uh…my daughter is in love and getting married." Callie managed to hiccup through her tears and, burying her nose in his flannel shirt, she sank into him. "I'm so happy, and I just wanted to tell you."

Stroking her back, Mason buried his face in her hair and, somehow, knew what she needed him to do.

He just held her.

* * * * *

Find out if Callie can really stay away from Mason, or if hot kisses and phone sex mean that friendship will be the last thing on their minds...

And for DJ, her on-again, off-again hookup is back in Boston for good. When her fantasy man becomes part of her everyday life, will it lead to love...or heartbreak?

Don't miss the next LOVE IN BOSTON *story, available October 2018!*

From New York Times *bestselling author Maisey Yates comes the sizzling second book in her new* GOLD VALLEY *Western romance series. Shy tomboy Kaylee Capshaw never thought she'd have a chance of winning the heart of her longtime friend Bennett Dodge, even if he is the cowboy of her dreams.*

But when she learns he's suddenly single, can she finally prove to him that the woman he's been waiting for has been right here all along?

Read on for a sneak peek at
UNTAMED COWBOY,
the latest in New York Times
bestselling author Maisey Yates's
GOLD VALLEY *series!*

CHAPTER ONE

KAYLEE CAPSHAW NEEDED a new life. Which was why she was steadfastly avoiding the sound of her phone vibrating in her purse while the man across from her at the beautifully appointed dinner table continued to talk, oblivious to the internal war raging inside of her.

Do not look at your phone.

The stern internal admonishment didn't help. Everything in her was still seized up with adrenaline and anxiety over the fact that she had texts she wasn't looking at.

Not because of her job. Any and all veterinary emergencies were being covered by her new assistant at the clinic, Laura, so that she could have this date with Michael, the perfectly nice man she was now ignoring while she warred within herself to *not look down at her phone*.

No. It wasn't work texts she was itching to look at.

But what if it was Bennett?

Laura knew that she wasn't supposed to interrupt

Kaylee tonight, because Kaylee was on a date, but she had conveniently not told Bennett. Because she didn't want to talk to Bennett about her dating anyone.

Mostly because she didn't want to hear if Bennett was dating anyone. If the woman lasted, Kaylee would inevitably know all about her. So there was no reason—in her mind—to rush into all of that.

She wasn't going to look at her phone.

"Going over the statistical data for the last quarter was really very interesting. It's fascinating how the holidays inform consumers."

Kaylee blinked. "What?"

"Sorry. I'm probably boring you. The corporate side of retail at Christmas is probably only interesting to people who work in the industry."

"Not at all," she said. Except, she wasn't interested. But she was trying to be. "How exactly did you get involved in this job living here?"

"Well, I can do most of it online. Sometimes I travel to Portland, which is where the corporate office is." Michael worked for a world-famous brand of sports gear, and he did something with the sales. Or data.

Her immediate attraction to him had been his dachshund, Clarence, whom she had seen for a tooth abscess a couple of weeks earlier. Then on a follow-up visit he had asked if Kaylee would like to go out, and she had honestly not been able to think of one good reason she shouldn't. Except for Bennett Dodge. Her best friend since junior high and the obsessive focus of her hormones since she'd discovered what men and women did together in the dark.

Which meant she absolutely needed to go out with Michael.

Bennett couldn't be the excuse. Not anymore.

She had fallen into a terrible rut over the last couple of years while she and Bennett had gotten their clinic up and running. Work and her social life revolved around him. Social gatherings were all linked to him and to his family.

She'd lived in Gold Valley since junior high, and the friendships she'd made here had mostly faded since then. She'd made friends when she'd gone to school for veterinary medicine, but she and Bennett had gone together, and those friends were mostly mutual friends.

If they ever came to town for a visit, it included Bennett. If she took a trip to visit them, it often included Bennett.

The man was up in absolutely everything, and the effects of it had been magnified recently as her world had narrowed thanks to their mutually demanding work schedule.

That amount of intense, focused time with him never failed to put her in a somewhat pathetic emotional space.

Hence the very necessary date.

Then her phone started vibrating because it was ringing, and she couldn't ignore that. "I'm sorry," she said. "Excuse me."

It was Bennett. Her heart slammed into her throat. She

should not answer it. She really shouldn't. She thought that even while she was pressing the green accept button.

"What's up?" she asked.

"Calving drama. I have a breech one. I need some help."

Bennett sounded clipped and stressed. And he didn't stress easily. He delivered countless calves over the course of the season, but a breech birth was never good. If the rancher didn't call him in time, there was rarely anything that could be done.

And if Bennett needed some assistance, then the situation was probably pretty extreme.

"Where are you?" she asked, darting a quick look over to Michael and feeling like a terrible human for being marginally relieved by this interruption.

"Out of town at Dave Miller's place. Follow the driveway out back behind the house."

"See you soon." She hung up the phone and looked down at her half-finished dinner. "I am so sorry," she said, forcing herself to look at Michael's face. "There's a veterinary emergency. I have to go."

She stood up, collecting her purse and her jacket. "I really am sorry. I tried to cover everything. But my partner... It's a barnyard thing. He needs help."

Michael looked... Well, he looked understanding. And Kaylee almost wished that he wouldn't. That he would be mad so that she would have an excuse to storm off and never have dinner with him again. That he would be unreasonable in some fashion so that she could call the date experiment a loss and go back to making no attempts at a romantic life whatsoever.

But he didn't. "Of course," he said. "You can't let something happen to an animal just because you're on a dinner date."

"I really can't," she said. "I'm sorry."

She reached into her purse and pulled out a twenty-dollar bill. She put it on the table and offered an apologetic smile before turning and leaving. Before he didn't accept her contribution to the dinner.

She was not going to make him pay for the entire meal on top of everything.

"Have a good evening," the hostess said as Kaylee walked toward the front door of the restaurant. "Please dine with us again soon."

Kaylee muttered something and headed outside, stumbling a little bit when her kitten heel caught in a crack in the sidewalk. That was the highest heel she ever wore, since she was nearly six feet tall in flats, and towering over one's date was not the best first impression.

But she was used to cowgirl boots and not these spindly, fiddly things that hung up on every imperfection. They were impractical. How any woman walked around in stilettos was beyond her.

The breeze kicked up, reminding her that March could not be counted on for warm spring weather as the wind stung her bare legs. The cost of wearing a dress. Which also had her feeling pretty stupid right about now.

She always felt weird in dresses, owing that to her stick figure and excessive height. She'd had to be tough from an early age. With parents who ultimately ended up ignoring her existence, she'd had to be self-sufficient.

It had suited her to be a tomboy because spending time outdoors, running around barefoot and climbing trees, far away from the fight scenes her parents continually staged in their house, was better than sitting at home.

Better to pretend she didn't like lace and frills, since her bedroom consisted of a twin mattress on the floor and a threadbare afghan.

She'd had a friend when she was little, way before they'd moved to Gold Valley, who'd had the prettiest princess room on earth. Lace bedding, a canopy. Pink walls with flower stencils. She'd been so envious of it. She'd felt nearly sick with it.

But she'd just said she hated girlie things. And never invited that friend over ever.

And hey, she'd been built for it. Broad shoulders and stuff.

Sadly, she *wasn't* built for pretty dresses.

But she needed strength more, anyway.

She was thankful she had driven her own truck, which was parked not far down the street against the curb. First-date rule for her. Drive your own vehicle. In case you had to make a hasty getaway.

And apparently she had needed to make a hasty getaway, just not because Michael was a weirdo or anything.

No, he had been distressingly nice.

She mused on that as she got into the driver's seat and started the engine. She pulled away from the curb and headed out of town. Yes, he had been perfectly nice. Really, there had been nothing wrong with him. And she was a professional at finding things wrong with the men she went on dates with. A professional at finding excuses for why a second date couldn't possibly happen.

She was ashamed to realize now that she was hoping he would consider this an excuse not to make a second date with her.

That she had taken a phone call in the middle of dinner and then had run off.

A lot of people had trouble dating. But often it was for deep reasons they had trouble identifying.

Kaylee knew exactly why she had trouble dating.

It was because she was in love with her best friend, Bennett Dodge. And he was *not* in love with her.

She gritted her teeth.

She wasn't in love with Bennett. No. She wouldn't allow that. She had lustful feelings for Bennett, and she cared deeply about him. But she wasn't in love with him. She refused to let it be that. Not anymore.

That thought carried her over the gravel drive that led to the ranch, back behind the house, just as Bennett had instructed. The doors to the barn were flung open, the lights on inside, and she recognized Bennett's truck parked right outside.

She killed the engine and got out, then moved into the barn as quickly as possible.

"What's going on?" she asked.

Dave Miller was there, his arms crossed over his chest, standing back against the wall. Bennett had his hand on the cow's back. He turned to look at her, the overhead light in the barn seeming to shine a halo around his cowboy hat. That chiseled face that she knew so well but never failed to make her stomach go tight. He stroked the cow, his large, capable hands drawing her attention, as well as the muscles in his forearm. He was wearing a tight T-shirt that showed off the play of those muscles to perfection. His large biceps and the scars on his skin from various on-the-job injuries. He had a stethoscope draped over his shoulders, and something about that combination—rough-and-ready cowboy meshed with concerned veterinarian—was her very particular catnip.

"I need to get the calf out as quickly as possible, and I need to do it at the right moment. Too quickly and we're likely to crush the baby's ribs." She had a feeling he said that part for the benefit of the nervous-looking rancher standing off to the side.

Dave Miller was relatively new to town, having moved up from California a couple of years ago with fantasies of rural living. A small ranch for him and his wife's retirement had grown to a medium-sized one over the past year or so. And while the older man had a reputation for taking great care of his animals, he wasn't experienced at this.

"Where do you want me?" she asked, moving over to where Bennett was standing.

"I'm going to need you to suction the hell out of this thing as soon as I get her out." He appraised her. "Where were you?"

"It doesn't matter."

"You're wearing a dress."

She shrugged. "I wasn't at home."

He frowned. "Were you out?"

This was not the time for Bennett to go overly concerned big brother on her. It wasn't charming on a normal day, but it was even less charming when she'd just abandoned her date to help deliver a calf. "If I wasn't at home, I was out. Better put your hand up the cow, Bennett," she said, feeling testy.

Bennett did just that, checking to see that the cow was dilated enough for him to extract the calf. Delivering a breech animal like this was tricky business. They were going to have to pull the baby out, likely with the aid of a chain or a winch, but not *too* soon, which would injure the mother. And not too quickly, which would injure them both.

But if they went too slow, the baby cow would end up completely cut off from its oxygen supply. If that happened, it was likely to never recover.

"Ready," he said. "I need chains."

She looked around and saw the chains lying on the ground, then she picked them up and handed them over. He grunted and pulled, producing the first hint of the calf's hooves. Then he lashed the chain around them. He began to pull again, his muscles straining against the fabric of his black T-shirt, flexing as he tugged hard.

She had been a vet long enough that she was inured to things like this, from a gross-out-factor perspective. But still, checking out a guy in the midst of all of this was probably a little imbalanced. Of course, that was the nature of how things were with her and Bennett.

They'd met when she'd moved to Gold Valley at thirteen—all long limbs, anger and adolescent awkwardness. And somehow, they'd fit. He'd lost his mother when he was young, and his family was limping along. Her own home life was hard, and she'd been desperate for escape from her parents' neglect and drunken rages at each other.

She never had him over. She didn't want to be at her house. She never wanted him, or any other friend, to see the way her family lived.

To see her sad mattress on the floor and her peeling nightstand.

Instead, they'd spent time at the Dodge ranch. His family had become hers, in many ways. They weren't perfect, but there was more love in their broken pieces than Kaylee's home had ever had.

He'd taught her to ride horses, let her play with the barn cats and the dogs that lived on the ranch. Together, the two of them had saved a baby squirrel that had been thrown out of his nest, nursing him back to health slowly in a little shoebox.

She'd blossomed because of him. Had discovered her love of animals. And had discovered she had the power to fix some of the broken things in the world.

The two of them had decided to become veterinarians together after they'd successfully saved the squirrel. And Bennett had never wavered.

He was a constant. A sure and steady port in the storm of life.

And when her feelings for him had started to shift and turn into more, she'd done her best to push them down because he was her whole world, and she didn't want to risk that by introducing anything as volatile as romance.

She'd seen how that went. Her parents' marriage was a reminder of just how badly all that could sour. It wasn't enough to make her swear off men, but it was enough to make her want to keep her relationship with Bennett as it was.

But that didn't stop the attraction.

If it were as simple as deciding not to want him, she would have done it a long time ago. And if it were as simple as being with another man, that would have worked back in high school when she had committed to finding herself a prom date and losing her virginity so she could get over Bennett Dodge already.

It had not worked. And the sex had been disappointing.

So here she was, fixating on his muscles while he helped an animal give birth.

Maybe there wasn't a direct line between those two things, but sometimes it felt like it. If all other men could just…not be so disappointing in comparison to Bennett Dodge, things would be much easier.

She looked away from him, making herself useful,

gathering syringes and anything she would need to clear
the calf of mucus that might be blocking its airway.
Bennett hadn't said anything, likely for Dave's benefit,
but she had a feeling he was worried about the health
of the heifer. That was why he needed her to see to the
calf as quickly as possible, because he was afraid he
would be giving treatment to its mother.

She spread a blanket out that was balled up and
stuffed in the corner—unnecessary, but it was something to do. Bennett strained and gave one final pull
and brought the calf down as gently as possible onto
the barn floor.

"There he is," Bennett said, breathing heavily.
"There he is."

His voice was filled with that rush of adrenaline that
always came when they worked jobs like this.

She and Bennett ran the practice together, but she
typically held down the fort at the clinic and treated
smaller domestic animals like birds, dogs, cats and the
occasional ferret.

Bennett worked with large animals, cows, horses,
goats and sometimes llamas. They had a mobile unit
for things like this.

But when push came to shove, they helped each other
out.

And when push came to pulling a calf out of its
mother, they definitely helped each other.

Bennett took care of the cord and then turned his
focus back to the mother.

Kaylee moved to the calf, who was glassy-eyed and

not looking very good. But she knew from her limited experience with this kind of delivery that just because they came out like this didn't mean they wouldn't pull through.

She checked his airway, brushing away any remaining mucus that was in the way. She put her hand back over his midsection and tried to get a feel on his heartbeat. "Bennett," she said, "stethoscope?"

"Here," he said, taking it from around his neck and tossing it her direction. She caught it and slipped the ear tips in, then pressed the diaphragm against the calf, trying to get a sense of what was happening in there.

His heartbeat sounded strong, which gave her hope.

His breathing was still weak. She looked around at the various tools, trying to see something she might be able to use. "Dave," she said to the man standing back against the wall. "I need a straw."

"A straw?"

"Yes. I've never tried this before, but I hear it works."

She had read that sticking a straw up a calf's nose irritated the system enough that it jolted them into breathing. And she hoped that was the case.

Dave returned quickly with the item that she had requested, and Kaylee moved the straw into position. Not gently, since that would defeat the purpose.

You had to love animals to be in her line of work. And unfortunately, loving them sometimes meant hurting them.

The calf startled, then heaved, his chest rising and falling deeply before he started to breathe quickly.

Kaylee pulled the straw out and lifted her hands. "Thank God."

Bennett turned around, shifting his focus to the calf and away from the mother. "Breathing?"

"Breathing."

He nodded, wiping his forearm over his forehead. "Good." His chest pitched upward sharply. "I think Mom is going to be okay, too."

UNTAMED COWBOY
by New York Times *bestselling author*
Maisey Yates,
available July 2018 wherever
HQN Books and ebooks are sold.
www.Harlequin.com

SPECIAL EXCERPT FROM

♦ HARLEQUIN®

Desire

Wealthy Texas politician Chase Ferguson ended things with his ex to protect her. Yet now she's crashed his isolated vacation house in a snowstorm. And when a stormbound seduction has real-world repercussions, he must make a stand for what—and who—he truly believes in.

Read on for a sneak peek at
A Snowbound Scandal *by Jessica Lemmon,*
part of her **Dallas Billionaires Club** series!

Her mouth watered, not for the food, but for him.

Not why you came here, Miriam reminded herself sternly.

Yet here she stood. Chase had figured out—before she'd admitted it to herself—that she'd come here not only to give him a piece of her mind but also to give herself the comfort of knowing he'd had a home-cooked meal on Thanksgiving.

She balled her fist as a flutter of desire took flight between her thighs. She wanted to touch him. Maybe just once.

He pushed her wineglass closer to her. An offer.

An offer she wouldn't accept.

Couldn't accept.

She wasn't unlike Little Red Riding Hood, having run to the wrong house for shelter. Only in this case, the Big Bad Wolf wasn't dining on Red's beloved grandmother but Miriam's family's home cooking.

An insistent niggling warned her that she could be next—and hadn't this particular "wolf" already consumed her heart?

"So, I'm going to go."

When she grabbed her coat and stood, a warm hand grasped her much cooler one. Chase's fingers stroked hers before lightly squeezing, his eyes studying her for a long moment, his fork hovering over his unfinished dinner.

Finally, he said, "I'll see you out."

"That's not necessary."

He did as he pleased and stood, his hand on her lower back as he walked with her. Outside, the wind pushed against the front door, causing the wood to creak. She and Chase exchanged glances. Had she waited too long?

"For the record, I don't want you to leave."

What she'd have given to hear those words on that airfield ten years ago.

"I'll be all right."

"You can't know that." He frowned out of either concern or anger, she couldn't tell which.

"Stay." Chase's gray-green eyes were warm and inviting, his voice a time capsule back to not-so-innocent days. The request was siren-call sweet, but she'd not risk herself for it.

"No." She yanked open the front door, shocked when the howling wind shoved her back a few inches. Snow billowed in, swirling around her feet, and her now wet, cold fingers slipped from the knob.

Chase caught her, an arm looped around her back, and shoved the door closed with the flat of one palm. She hung there, suspended by the corded forearm at her back, clutching his shirt in one fist, and nearly drowned in his lake-colored eyes.

"I can stay for a while longer," she squeaked, the decision having been made for her.

His handsome face split into a brilliant smile.

Don't miss A Snowbound Scandal *by Jessica Lemmon,
part of her* **Dallas Billionaires Club** *series!*

*Available August 2018 wherever
Harlequin® Desire books and ebooks are sold.*

www.Harlequin.com

LOVE
Harlequin
romance?

Join our Harlequin community to share your thoughts and connect with other romance readers!

Be the first to find out about promotions, news, and exclusive content!

Sign up for the Harlequin e-newsletter and download a free book from any series at

www.TryHarlequin.com

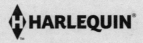

THE WORLD IS BETTER WITH

Romance

Harlequin has everything from contemporary, passionate and heartwarming to suspenseful and inspirational stories.

Whatever your mood, we have a romance just for you!

ne bo
you!

Earn points from all your Harlequin book
purchases from wherever you shop.

Turn your points into *FREE BOOKS* of your choice
OR
EXCLUSIVE GIFTS from your favorite
authors or series.

Join for FREE today at
www.HarlequinMyRewards.com.

Harlequin My Rewards is a free program (no fees)
without any commitments or obligations.

MYR17